Beowulf Sheehan

Maria Dahvana Headley
BEOWULF

Maria Dahvana Headley is a #1 *New York Times*–bestselling author and editor. Her books include the novels *The Mere Wife*, *Magonia*, *Aerie*, and *Queen of Kings*, and the memoir *The Year of Yes*. With Neil Gaiman, she is the coeditor of *Unnatural Creatures*. Her stories have been short-listed for the Shirley Jackson, Nebula, and World Fantasy Awards.

BEOWULF

MCD x FSG Originals

Farrar, Straus and Giroux

New York

BEOWULF

A NEW TRANSLATION **MARIA DAHVANA HEADLEY**

MCD × FSG Originals
Farrar, Straus and Giroux
120 Broadway, New York 10271

Library of Congress Cataloging-in-Publication Data
Names: Headley, Maria Dahvana, 1977– author.
Title: Beowulf : a new translation / Maria Dahvana Headley.
Other titles: Beowulf. English.
Description: First edition. | New York : MCD × FSG Originals ; Farrar,
    Straus and Giroux, 2020.
Identifiers: LCCN 2020012283 | ISBN 9780374110031 (pbk.)
Subjects: LCGFT: Poetry.
Classification: LCC PS3608.E233 B46 2020 | DDC 811/.6—dc23
LC record available at https://lccn.loc.gov/2020012283

Our books may be purchased in bulk for promotional, educational, or
business use. Please contact your local bookseller or the Macmillan
Corporate and Premium Sales Department at 1-800-221-7945, extension
5442, or by e-mail at MacmillanSpecialMarkets@macmillan.com.

www.fsgoriginals.com • www.fsgbooks.com
Follow us on Twitter, Facebook, and Instagram at @fsgoriginals

10 9 8 7

For Grimoire William Gwenllian Headley,

who gestated alongside this book,

changing the way I thought about love, bloodfeuds,

woman-warriors, and *wyrd*.

My love affair with *Beowulf* began with Grendel's mother, the moment I encountered her in an illustrated compendium of monsters,* a slithery greenish entity standing naked in a swamp, knife in hand. I was about eight, and on the hunt for any sort of woman-warrior. Wonder Woman and She-Ra were fine, but Grendel's mother was better. She had a ferocious look and seemed to give precisely zero fucks, not that I had that language to describe her at that point in my life. In the book I first saw her in, there was no Grendel, no Beowulf, no fifty years a queen. She was just a woman with a weapon, all by herself in the center of the page. I imagined she was the point of whatever story she came from. When I finally encountered the actual poem, years later, I was appalled to discover that Grendel's mother was not only not the main event

---

* I wish I could tell you which compendium of monsters it was. Hunts have revealed two images that may have been conflated into the version I remember. Brian Froud and Alan Lee's *Faeries* (New York: Harry N. Abrams, Inc., 1978) contains an assortment of eldritch figures from English folklore, among them the nightmare-provoking two-page spread of

but also, to many people, an extension of Grendel rather than a character unto herself, despite the significant ink devoted to her fighting capabilities. It aggravated me enough that I eventually wrote a contemporary adaptation of *Beowulf*—*The Mere Wife*, a novel in which the Grendel's mother character is a protagonist, a PTSD-stricken veteran of the United States' wars in the Middle East. That might have been the end of it, but by that point I'd tumbled head over heels into *Beowulf* itself, and was, like everyone who ever translates it, obsessed.

It's a somewhat unlikely object of obsession, this thousand-ish-year-old epic. *Beowulf* bears the distinction of appearing to be basic—one man, three battles, lots of gold—while actually being an intricate treatise on morality, mascu-

---

Jenny Greenteeth and Peg Powler, both child-eating greenish river hags, each depicted solo, partially immersed. Neither of these align wholly with my memory (they're unarmed), but they're similar to other (monstrous) depictions of Grendel's mother. However, I grew up in a house full of art books; my mother's a painter. J. R. Skelton's illustration of Grendel's mother, from *Stories of Beowulf* (1908), depicts a greenish, profoundly muscular warrior-woman kneeling atop a golden-armored Beowulf, raising her *seax* to slay him. It's very much like paintings of the heroic Judith (beheading Holofernes and posing with her sword) I saw around the same time, and it's possible that all these ingredients converged into the Grendel's mother I remember. On a less literary, but incidentally very Beowulf-related note, add some Sigourney Weaver (*Alien*, 1979) to this. All that said, I spent a lot of my childhood in library corners, looking at books no one knew I was looking at. It's still possible the image I remember exists out there somewhere. If you find it, let me know.

linity, flexibility, and failure. It's 3,182 lines of alliterative wildness, a sequence of monsters and would-be heroes. In it, multiple old men try to plot out how to retire in a world that offers no retirement. Hoarders of all kinds attempt to maintain control of people, halls, piles of gold, and even the volume of the natural world. Queens negotiate for the survival of their sons, attempt to save their children by marrying themselves to warriors, and, in one case, battle for vengeance on their son's murderers. Graying old men long for one last exam to render them heroes once and for all. The phrase "That was a good king" recurs throughout the poem, because the poem is fundamentally concerned with how to get and keep the title "Good." The suspicion that at any moment a person might shift from hero into howling wretch, teeth bared, causes characters ranging from scops to ring-lords to drop cautionary anecdotes. Does fame keep you good? No. Does gold keep you good? No. Does your good wife keep you good? No. What keeps you good? Vigilance. That's it. And even with vigilance, even with courage, you still might go forth to slay a dragon (or, if you're Grendel, slay a Dane), die in the slaying, and leave everyone and everything you love vulnerable. The world of the poem—a fantastical version of Denmark in the fifth to early sixth century and the land of the Geats, in present-day Sweden—is distant, but the actions of the poem's characters are familiar.

As much as *Beowulf* is a poem about Then, it's also (and

always has been) a poem about Now, and how we got here. The poem is, after all, a poem about willfully blinkered privilege, about the shock and horror of experiencing discomfort when one feels entitled to luxury.

There are many translations out there, enough that you could read one a day for months and not repeat. They make up a startlingly diverse corpus of interpretations and styles, with the occasional screeching veer into new plot points. (How about the transgressive and fairly persuasive notion that the last survivor of a forgotten tribe, in burying his people's gold, transforms by curse into the dragon?)* Every English-language translator's take on how to translate this text is motivated by different ideas of how to use modern English to convey things inexpressible in it.

This translation, for example, was completed during the first months of my son's life. Parenting a baby is listening to someone use a language in which certain sounds mean a slew of things, and one must rely heavily on context to gain clarity;

---

* This tempting theory is from Raymond Tripp's "The Dragon King of *Beowulf*," published in 2005 in *In Geardagum*, and also dealt with in *More About the Fight with the Dragon* (Lanham, MD: University Press of America, 1983). It's not unprecedented. In Iceland's *Volsunga Saga*, Fafnir starts out a dwarf and ends up becoming a dragon due to cursed gold. Perhaps, for a translator, more pragmatically, shape-shifting the last survivor into the dragon makes sense of difficult pronouns in that section, which create consistent bafflement about which character is being referenced—the dragon, the last survivor, or the thief.

a language in which there is no way to translate accurately the ancient sound that means "hungry," because, to the preverbal speaker, the sound means and is used to signal a compendium of things, something more like "belly hurt—longing—breast—empty mouth—bottle—swallow—milk—help."

While this gloss is somewhat tongue-in-cheek, it's not far from the actuality of Old English translation. It's possible to make a case for more than one definition of many words, and the challenge is to land on an interpretation that braids rationally into the narrative, without translating a male warrior into a bear, or a woman warrior into a literal sea wolf rather than a metaphoric one.* You must choose wisely, and then,

---

* I do think both those interpretations are incorrect, but one of them is a generally accepted truth of text, a supporting argument for monstrosity in Grendel's mother. The other interpretation would these days be considered an embarrassing, though delightful, error—almost no one thinks that by *beorn*, and indeed by "Beowulf," as in "Bee-Wolf," as in "honey-eater," as in "Bear," the poet meant Beowulf to be (even partially) a bragging, talkative bear (never mind our hero's supernatural strength and capacity to swim long distances, dive, and hold his breath for a full day). It'd be fun, though: an armored, perpetually unwed bear, a predecessor of Philip Pullman's *panserbjørne*, especially in a narrative already populated with wonders. Friedrich Panzer's (no relation to Iorek Byrnison's tribe) 1910 Bear's Son thesis, surveying possible folkloric lineage for the *Beowulf* story, is a highly recommended storyzone. And if we felt like it, we could wander for a long time in bear cult ties (check out Richard Neal Coffin's 1962 PhD dissertation, "*Beowulf* and its Relationship to Norse and Finno-Ugric Beliefs and Narratives," Boston University; in warriors buried on bearskins with hounds and gold beside them; in notions of Beowulf-as-stealth-berserker.

somehow, structure those wise (or frustrated) choices into poetry.

With this text, perfection is impossible. The poem was written in the language we now call Old English, sometime between the mid-seventh and the end of the tenth centuries, and exists in a lone manuscript copy, the Nowell Codex. The version contained therein was written down sometime between AD 975 and 1025, by two scribes, A and B, with different handwriting and different tendencies toward error. Add to this the fact that the manuscript isn't intact: bits of poem were lost over the centuries—first in the gestation of the written version itself, which was at the mercy of memory and (presumably) mead, and later, in a library fire in 1731, which badly singed the edges of the manuscript. It was rebound in the late nineteenth century, and in the interim, its edges crumbled beyond resurrection. Worms feasted. Least visibly and most significantly, scribal emendations changed the nature of the story in both subtle and unsubtle ways.* Gaps were

---

* In the original manuscript, for example, Scribe A wrote that Grendel was doomed because he was descended from *chames cynne*—or "Ham's kin." That got scratched out, presumably by Scribe B, and replaced with *caines cynne*, "Cain's kin." Subsequent references to Abel make a case for that palimpsestic edit, and for the curse—which makes of Cain a fugitive wanderer. Grendel, of course, isn't a wanderer. His (and his mother's) home address is well known to Hrothgar, so he's not exactly a fugitive, either. Biblically, Ham's kin also got cursed, because Noah's son Ham saw a drunken, naked Noah (it's up for grabs what that "seeing" actually consisted of), and so Noah cursed Ham's kin with servitude. The notion of

plugged with metric maybes, and lacunae inserted into lines that appear whole, to make sense of shifts in tone. All this is to say that *Beowulf* has been wrangled with, wrung out, and reworked for centuries. It's been written upon almost as much by translators and librarians as it was by the original poet(s) and scribes.

The original *Beowulf* was composed by an author who imagined a world in which a monster is infuriated by loud music, a dragon ripples luxuriously about beloved gold, an elderly woman is able to make viable physical war against all the king's men, and a young warrior can hold his breath for a full day while fighting sea monsters, winning his battle only because God shines a spotlight on a slaying sword. A "perfect" translation would require the translator to time travel fantastically rather than historically—more Narnia than *Bill & Ted's Excellent Adventure*. As if this weren't enough, the

---

Noah's curse on Ham persevered over the centuries into the still-cited American insistence that slavery is ideologically justified by the Bible, and onward into the potential queerness of Ham being justification for homophobia. Two for one Biblical bias support! Notions of othering lineage may be applied to Grendel either way, but the two curses, while often conflated, are different. One curse makes of Grendel a fugitive, the other, a slave. Neither gives us the full story of Grendel's grievance, but the cursed lineage has often been used to simplify Grendel's identity through association, rendering him irrationally and indubitably evil, rather than someone provoked by specific Danes. For more on this topic, see Toni Morrison's "Grendel and His Mother," collected in *The Source of Self-Regard: Selected Essays, Speeches, and Meditations* (New York: Alfred K. Knopf, 2019).

language of the poem is as much a world-building tool as the plot is, engineered with the poet's own anachronistic filter, an archaic, lyric lexicography.*

"If you wish to translate, not re-write, *Beowulf*," J.R.R. Tolkien wrote in 1940, "your language must be literary and traditional: not because it is now a long while since the poem was made, or because it speaks of things that have since become ancient; but because the diction of *Beowulf* was poetical, archaic, artificial (if you will), in the day the poem was made."†

Tolkien and I wouldn't have agreed when it comes to the sort of language required for a translation of *Beowulf*—perceptions of "literary" and "traditional" language vary widely depending on who's doing the perceiving, and Tolkien

---

* And who was this poet, anyway? No one knows. Someone alive at some point in a three-century swath, someone (probably) in England, (probably) not a woman, but again, who knows? The poet was certainly a genius; genius defies gender. The idea that there are only a couple of poems in the Old English corpus that could plausibly have been written by female poets (specifically "The Wife's Lament" and "Wulf and Eadwacer," both because of POV) is a ridiculous one. The notion that women write only about women's business is equally ridiculous—as indeed is the idea that there is such a circumscribable arena as "women's business" at all. A wonderful thing one learns when one writes about imaginary kingdoms for a living is that, in fact, anyone can imagine anything, and if the writer is good, they can do it persuasively.

† "On Translating *Beowulf*," collected in *The Monsters and the Critics, and Other Essays* (New York: HarperCollins, 2006).

had a liking for the courtly that I do not share—but we agree that the original's dense wordplay must be reckoned with.

Amid a slew of regressions in the past half decade, I must cite a win—the democratization of information. Access to formerly gate-kept texts has been radically broadened. Until recently, it was a cotton-gloved privilege to view the original manuscript of *Beowulf*. Now a click, and there you are, looking at handwriting a thousand years old: "*Hwæt. We Gardena in geardagum, þeodcyninga, þrym gefrunon . . .*" Not only is the original accessible to anyone with an internet connection, so are a huge number of translations and volumes of evolving scholarship, many long out of print. This translation exists because of that access.

It is both pleasurable and desirable to read more than one translation of this poem, because when it comes to translating *Beowulf*, there is no sacred clarity. What the translated text says is a matter of study, interpretation, and poetic leaps of faith. Every translator translates this poem differently. That's part of its glory.

And so, I offer to the banquet table this translation, done by an American woman born in the year 1977, a person who grew up surrounded by sled dogs, coyotes, rattlesnakes, and bubbling natural hot springs nestled in the wild high desert of Idaho, a person who, if we were looking at the poem's categories, would fall much closer in original habitat to Grendel and his mother than to Beowulf or even the lesser denizens of Hrothgar's court.

I came to this project as a novelist, interested specifically in rendering the story continuously and clearly, while also creating a text that feels as bloody and juicy as I think it ought to feel. Despite its reputation to generations of unwilling students, forced as freshmen into arduous translations, *Beowulf* is a living text in a dead language, the kind of thing meant to be shouted over a crowd of drunk celebrants. Even though it was probably written down in the quiet confines of a scriptorium, *Beowulf* is not a quiet poem. It's a dazzling, furious, funny, vicious, desperate, hungry, beautiful, mutinous, maudlin, supernatural, rapturous shout.

In contrast to the methods of some previous translators, I let the poem's story lead me to its style. The lines in this translation were structured for speaking, and for speaking in contemporary rhythms. The poets I'm most interested in are those who use language as instrument, inventing words and creating forms as necessary, in the service of voice. I come from the land of cowboy poets, and while theirs is not the style I used for this translation, I did spend a lot of time imagining the narrator as an old-timer at the end of the bar, periodically pounding his glass and demanding another. *I saw it with my own eyes.*

A brief and general word about meter and style tropes:

early English verse is distinguished by both alliteration and stress patterns over a caesura (in oral versions, the caesura is a pause—on the page, a gap between the two halves of a line). Each half line contains two stressed syllables; the two stressed syllables in the first half line alliterate with the first stressed syllable in the second. Rhyme is used in *Beowulf*, but less predictably. It's typically used to emphasize sequences—waves crashing against a shore, for example. And stylistically, *Beowulf* employs a variety of compound words, or kennings, to poetically describe both the commonplace and the astounding. Hence, we've got some wonderful and distinctive things: "whale-road" for sea; "battle-sweat" for blood; "sky-candle" for sun.

Like everyone who's ever translated this text, I had some fun. After reading a variety of translations mimicking early English meter, and attempting a version myself, I decided that corpse-littered hill wasn't one I wished to die on. Likewise, attempts to translate this text into other meters, which have typically yielded inadvertent hilarity. At some point, I encountered A. Diedrich Wackerbarth's 1849 ballad translation,* here quoted in the introduction of Grendel's mother:

---

* Read Chauncey B. Tinker's exuberantly claws-out *The Translations of Beowulf: A Critical Bibliography* (New York: Henry Holt and Company, 1903) for a catalog and critique of *Beowulf* translations, verse, prose, fragments, and paraphrases up to 1902. Of Wackerbarth's translation, Tinker

The mother Fiend, a Soul had she
Blood-greedy like the Gallows-tree,
And she for deadly Vengeance' Sake
Will now the Battle undertake.

I didn't desire to graft peach branches to a cactus, or vice versa, and so I gave myself leave to play with all the traditional aspects, preserving many kennings and inventing some of my own, while also employing the sensibilities of a modern poet rather than an ancient one. This translation rhymes in a variety of ways, including the occasional heroic couplet. I love raucous rhyme schemes and rampant alliteration, and the near universally derided line from John Richard Clark Hall's 1901 translation, "ten timorous troth-breakers," delights me. Sure, it's undignified; sure, it's nasty—but so are the runaway warriors it references. My alliteration (and embedded rhyme) often rolls over line breaks, which would be forbidden in early English metric rules. In this translation, though, I wanted the feeling of linguistic links throughout.

---

shudders: "It would seem that if there were a measure less suited to the *Beowulf* style than the Miltonic blank verse used by Conybeare, it would be the ballad measures used by Wackerbarth. The movement of the ballad is easy, rapid, and garrulous. Now, if there are three qualities of which the *Beowulf* is not possessed, they are ease, rapidity, and garrulity . . . But there is still another reason for shunning them. They are almost continuously suggestive of [Sir Walter] Scott. Of all men else the translator of *Beowulf* should avoid Scott" (48).

The poem employs time passing and regressing, future predictions, quick History 101s, neglected bits of necessary information flung, as needed, into the tale. The original reads, at least in some places, like Old English freestyle, and in others like the wedding toast of a drunk uncle who's suddenly remembered a poem he memorized at boarding school.

There are noble characters in *Beowulf*, but the poem itself is not noble. There is elevated language in *Beowulf*, but the poem feels populist. It's entertaining, episodic, and full of wonders. As I constructed the persona of the narrator, other things about the poem fell into place—the insistent periodic recaps for a distracted multinight audience, the epithets and adamant character calibrations interspersed throughout ("That was a good king"). I emphasized those things where I found them, both for the mnemonic aid factor and for the feeling of a communal, colloquial history.

There has been much debate about the level to which the translated text should be archaized to emphasize for modern readers the alien landscape of early English verse, and specifically to what degree translators should mimic the poet's own choice to use words already archaic and poetic at the time of the poem's composition. In some cases, the urge to archaize won soundly over the urge to make sense. Thus, there are plenty of crinolined "forsooth" and "ween" ridden translations to choose from, should the reader be so inclined, as well as a series of Scots-tinged selections: "mickle" has tempted many, as has a hunger for "twixt," and though much of this is attested in the Old English, in translation one can easily devolve into a peculiar Elizabethan pastiche.

Given that both poetic voice and communicative clarity are my interests here, my diction reflects access to the entirety of the English word-hoard—some of these words legitimately archaic or underknown ("corse," "sere," "sclerite"), others recently written into lexicons of slang or thrown up by new cultural contexts ("swole," "stan," "hashtag: blessed"), and already fading into, if not obscurity, uncertain status. Language is a living thing, and when it dies, it leaves bones. I dropped some fossils here, next to some newborns. I'm as interested in contemporary idiom and slang as I am in the archaic. There are other translations if you're looking for the language of courtly romance and knights. This one has "life-tilt" and "rode hard . . . stayed thirsty" in it.

Back I come, for that reason, to *hwæt*. It's been translated many ways. "Listen." "Hark." "Lo." Seamus Heaney translated it as "So," an attention-getting intonation, taken from the memory of his Irish uncle telling tales at the table.*

I come equipped with my own memories of sitting at the bar's end listening to men navigate darts, trivia, and women, and so, in this book, I translate it as "Bro." The entire poem,

---

* See Heaney's wonderful introduction to his *Beowulf: A New Verse Translation* (New York: Farrar, Straus and Giroux, 1999).

and especially the monologues of the men in it, feels to me like the sort of competitive conversations I've often heard between men, one insisting on his right to the floor while simultaneously insisting that he's friendly. "Bro" is, to my ear, a means of commanding attention while shuffling focus calculatedly away from hierarchy.

Depending on tone, "bro" can render you family or foe. The poem is about that notion, too. Marital pacts are made and catastrophes ensue, kingdoms are offered and rejected, familial bonds are ensured not with blood, but with gold. When I use "bro" elsewhere in the poem, whether in the voice of Beowulf, Hrothgar, or the narrator, it's to keep us thinking of the ways that family can be sealed by formulation, the ways that men can afford (or deny) one another power and safety by using coded language, and erase women from power structures by speaking collegially only to other men.

There's another way of using "bro," of course, and that is as a means of satirizing a certain form of inflated, overconfident, aggressive male behavior. I think the poet's own language sometimes does that, periodically weighing in with commentary about how the men in the poem think all is well, but have discerned nothing about blood relatives' treachery and their own heathen helplessness. Is this text attempting to be a manual for successful masculinity? No, although at a glance it appears to be a hero story. *Beowulf* is a manual for how to live as a man, if you are, in fact, more like the monsters than the men. It's about taming wild, solitary appetites, and about the failure to tame them. It is not, in the poet's opinion, entirely to Beowulf's credit that he continues wild and solitary into old age. Compare him with another old man, Ongentheow, whose long-form story is told by the messenger bringing ill tidings to Beowulf's people after Beowulf's death. That old man, though an enemy to the Geats, is depicted as responsible to his wife, children, and people, battling strategically on their behalf, thinking of their safety even as he is cornered and killed. The humans in *Beowulf* are communal, battling together, leaders alongside lesser-ranked warriors. Those who are superhuman (or supernatural)— Grendel, his mother, the dragon, and Beowulf—battle solo and are ultimately weakened by their wild solitude.

There's a geomythological theory that the larger-than-life men in this poem—Hygelac, mentioned in other texts as a giant; Beowulf; Grendel—came into the poetic imagination due to medieval discoveries of fossilized mammoth bones, which, when incorrectly reassembled, look like nothing so much as tremendous human skeletons.* The theory is tempting in a variety of ways, among them the notion that these giant men were literally made of monsters. These physical "mistranslations" bear some similarity to the poem's con-

---

* See: Timothy J. Burbery, "Fossil Folklore in the *Liber Monstrorum*, *Beowulf*, and Medieval Scholarship," *Folklore* 126, no. 3 (2015). See also:

struct (and interrogation) of impervious masculinity. An emotional wound can send a previously powerful man into a swift, suicidal tailspin. See Hrethel and Hrothgar, and even Beowulf, rushing solo at a dragon, attempting to prove himself to an audience of young men who turn out to be mostly cowards.

Beowulf is usually seen as a masculine text, but I think that's somewhat unfair. The poem, while (with one exception) not structured around the actions of women, does contain extensive portrayals of motherhood and peace-weaving marital compromise, female warriors, and speculation on what it means to lose a son. In this translation, I worked to shine a light on the motivations, actions, and desires of the poem's female characters, as well as to clarify their identities. While there are many examples of gendered inequality in the poem, there is no shortage of female power.

Grendel's mother, my original impetus for involvement with this text, is almost always depicted in translation as an obvious monster rather than as a human woman—and her monstrosity doesn't typically allow even for partial humanity, though the poem itself shows us that she lives in a hall, uses weapons, is trained in combat, and follows blood-feud rules.

Adrienne Mayor, *The First Fossil Hunters: Dinosaurs, Mammoths, and Myth in Greek and Roman Times* (Princeton, NJ: Princeton University Press, 2001).

"Ogress . . . inhuman troll-wife" —Tolkien, 1926,
   published 2014
"That female horror . . . hungry fiend" —Raffel, 1963
"Ugly troll-lady" —Trask, 1997
"Monstrous hell-bride . . . swamp-thing from hell"
   —Heaney, 1999

It makes some sense that she'd be translated that way. Her son, Grendel, eats people and can carry home a doggie bag full of warriors. It's just the two of them living in their under-mere hall, and for many late nineteenth- and early twentieth-century translators of this text, it would only have followed for the monstrous portion of Grendel's parentage to be his mother rather than his absentee father. For most of those translators, the difficulty of imagining a human woman fully armed, fully elderly (she's been ruler of her kingdom as long as Hrothgar's been ruler of his), would have been insurmountable. There are other explanations for monsterhood in Grendel's mother, of course—some interesting ones. I'm somewhat persuaded by adjacent lore surrounding troll-transformation due to rape,* if only because the poisonous myth that a raped woman is a

---

* For more on this, see the wonderfully titled chapter "Bone-Crones Have No Hearth: Some Women in the Medieval Wilderness," by Marijane Osborn and Gillian R. Overing, in *Textures of Place: Exploring Humanist Geographies* (Minneapolis: University of Minnesota Press, 2001). See also: Osborn's original poem "Grendel's Mother Broods Over Her Feral Son," *Old English Newsletter* 39, no. 3 (2006), based on a 1914 scrap

ruined woman, thus an abomination and thus, all too possibly, evil, has persisted as long as women have. Grendel's father is an unknown. That said, though, Grendel's mother doesn't behave like a monster. She behaves like a bereaved mother who happens to have a warrior's skill.

The tradition of monstrous depiction assisted by monstrous physical descriptors persevered in translation (though not necessarily in scholarship) into the later years of the twentieth century and beyond, particularly after Frederick Klaeber's 1922 glossary defined the word used to reference Grendel's mother, *aglaec-wif*, as "wretch, or monster, of a woman." Never mind that *aglaec-wif* is merely the feminine form of *aglaeca*, which Klaeber defines as "hero" when applied to Beowulf, and "monster, demon, fiend" when referencing Grendel, his mother, and the dragon. *Aglaeca* is used elsewhere in early English to refer both to Sigemund and to the Venerable Bede, and in those contexts, it's likelier to mean something akin to "formidable." Fair enough. Multiple meanings to Old English words, after all.

Grendel's mother is referred to in the poem as "*ides, aglaec-wif*," which means, given this logic, "formidable noblewoman."

---

of philological interpretation by William A. P. Sewell, the notion that Scyld Scefing decimated the Ereli, the tallest people of Scandinavia, who "fought like wild beasts." In Osborn's poem, Grendel's mother is part of that massacred tribe, and Grendel's father, by rape, is Scyld's descendant the Halfdane, making Grendel brother to Hrothgar, and Grendel's war on Heorot Hall an act of blood-feud vengeance. Also, the poem is in Grendel's mother's voice, which is reason enough to read it.

She isn't physically described, beyond that she looks like a woman, and is tall. The Old English word for fingers, *fingrum*, has frequently been translated as "claws," but Grendel's mother fights effectively with a knife, and wielding a knife while also possessing long nails is—as anyone who's ever had a manicure knows—a near impossibility. The word *brimwylf*, or "sea-wolf," is also used as a supporting argument for monstrosity, but it's a guess. The manuscript itself reads *brimwyl*, which may have been meant to be *brimwif*. Elsewhere, Grendel's mother is referred to as a *merewif*, or "ocean-woman," so it's very possible that scribal error introduced a wolf where a wife should be, and that traditions of gendered hierarchy made a monster of a mother. In any case, "sea-wolf" is a poetic term, and might be as easily applied to Beowulf as it is to Grendel's mother. In *Beowulf*, it seems likely to me that some translators, seeking to make their own sense of this story, have gone out of their way to bolster Beowulf's human credentials by amplifying the monstrosity of Grendel's mother, when in truth, the combatants are similar. They're both extraordinary fighters, and the battle between Beowulf and Grendel's mother is, unlike other battles in the poem, a battle of equally matched warriors. God's established soft spot for Beowulf is the deciding factor, not physical strength.

Ecgtheow's heir would've been filleted, recategorized as MIA, and left to rot in her cavern, had not his suit

saved him. That, too, was God's work.
The Lord, maker of miracles, sky-designer,
had no trouble leveling the playing field
when Beowulf beat the count and stood.

He glimpsed it hanging in her hoard, that armory
of heirlooms, somebody's birthright. A sword,
blessed by blood and flood . . .

The poet's depiction of Grendel's mother is complex: as admiring as it is critical. The proximity in the text of the heroic Hildeburh, whose narrative of loss and vengeance is only a step and a knife removed from Grendel's mother's story, isn't accidental. In terms of narrative balance, I'm interested in versions of the *Beowulf* story that emphasize Grendel's mother's right to recompense for the death of her son—early English feud rules allow blood for blood, and, in killing one of Hrothgar's advisers, Grendel's mother exacts a legal revenge. Later in the story, Beowulf himself takes feud-rule vengeance for the death of his young king Heardred, arming rebels to eliminate Heardred's killer, Onela.

I don't know that Grendel's mother should be perceived in binary terms—monster versus human. My own experiences as a woman tell me it's very possible to be mistaken for monstrous when one is only doing as men do: providing for and defending oneself. Whether one's solitary status is a result of abandonment by a man or because of a choice, the reams of lore about single, self-sustaining women, and particularly about solitary elderly women, suggest that many human women have been, over the centuries, mistaken for supernatural creatures simply because they were alone and capable. For all these reasons, I've translated Grendel's mother here as "warrior-woman," "outlaw," and "reclusive night-queen."

Throughout the poem, I've also encouraged moments in which the feminine might already be poetically suggested. Thus, lines 1431–1439, wherein Hrothgar and Beowulf's men arrive at the mere and kill a sea monster, become:

> A Geat drew his bow and struck
> a slithering one. An arrow piercing its scales, it
> struggled
> and thrashed in the water. The other men, invigorated,
> sought to join the killing; a second shot, a third,
> then they slung themselves into the shallows
> and speared it. *This* monster they could control.
> They cornered it, clubbed it, tugged it onto the rocks,
> stillbirthed it from its mere-mother, deemed it
> damned,
> and made of it a miscarriage . . .

Similarly, in lines 1605–1610, as Beowulf discovers that the sword he's used to kill Grendel's mother is melting, I used the existing lines, which could suggest a literal defrosting of springs, to suggest a situation in which Spring is a captive, chained and released by God. There is plenty in the world history of pagan seasonal myth to support such a reading, and similar references to captivity and power abound in the poem, including in the scene these lines are from:

> Below, in Beowulf's hands, the slaying-sword
> began to melt like ice, just as the world thaws
> in May when the Father unlocks the shackles
> that've chained frost to the climate, and releases
> hostage heat, uses sway over seasons to uncage
> His prisoner, Spring, and let her stumble into the sun.

I see the women in this story as part of a continuum of experience, just as the men are. Freawaru, the Bartered Beautiful Bride, who takes the first steps into a blood-wedding. Modthryth, the Bartered Bad Bride, who seeks preemptive vengeance on the world of men before entering an unexpectedly happy marriage. (Perhaps unsurprisingly, Modthryth is often the only character cut from children's versions of *Beowulf*.) Hygd, the Self-Bartering Bride, who attempts (and fails) to negotiate her son's survival by persuading Beowulf to ascend to kingship over him. Hildeburh, the Failed Peaceweaver, who incubates overwinter a yearning for vengeance, after her son, brother, and ultimately her husband are killed. Wealhtheow, the Canny Queen, who is often depicted as acquiescent. In fact, her speech to the hall during the post-Grendel celebration is a masterpiece of negotiation. Within her role as an obedient wife, she works the room to her own advantage, attempting to gain security for her sons from the hero her husband has become smitten with. I translated Wealhtheow's speech to clarify the threats I think have always been part of it. Grendel's Mother, the Un-Husbanded Warrior, who rules her own kingdom until she is elderly, losing her son, but succeeding in exacting bloody vengeance. To that coven, I've added the dragon,* curled about her hoard, her bedchamber invaded by someone seeking to burgle. Her vengeance for that theft lights the sky and land on fire. After vengeance comes grief. The last woman in the story is the Geatish woman, the Mourner, not mourning Beowulf so much as her own future without a king, new versions of old horrors—blood, swords, and men. That this occurs just prior to Beowulf's funerary tribute, his men repeating variations on "That was a good king," is no accident. Her agonized inclusion here renders that final round of tributes ironic.

In the end, *Beowulf* depicts edge-times and border wars, and we're in them still. As I write this introduction, and as I worked on this translation over the past few years, the world

---

* Often depicted as male, rather than as ungendered.

of the poem felt increasingly relevant. I regularly found myself muttering speeches written a thousand years ago as I watched their contemporary equivalents unfold on the news. This moment, and the moments before it, the centuries of colonialist impulse and kingdom-building, the peoples being built upon, are things that concerned the *Beowulf* poet and concern this translator, too.

The news cycle is filled with men Hrothgar's age failing utterly at self-awareness, and even going full Heremod. Politics twist paradoxically into ever more isolationist *and* interventionist corners, increasingly based in hoarding and horde-panic. The world, as ever, is filled with desolate places and glittering ones, sharing armed borders. Children are confiscated. Refugees are imprisoned. The people doing the imprisoning claim they're persecuting criminals, monsters, but some of those are infants, and most of those are running from worse wars in their own homelands. We are, some of us anyway, living the Geatish woman's lament, writ large.

In the United States of 2020, everyone, including small children, has the capacity to be as deadly as the spectacular warriors of this poem. The teeth, swords, and claws of the Old English epic have been converted into automatic possibilities, the power to slay thirty men in a minute no longer the genius of a select few but a purchasable perk of weapon ownership. The kings and dragons of the poem possess hoards akin to those of basic American households: iPhone idols, nonstick cookware, unused goblets counted by the dozen. Queen- and king-size beds for the queens and kings of small halls in the suburbs, fake feathers and swansdown like the reclaimed wings of minor monsters, bought and shipped overnight by Amazon Prime—itself a corporation named for a legendary tribe of female warriors, though in this case the title of warrior stands in for consumer convenience, sorcerous shipping speeds, access to the great, luxuriant, on-sale *everything*.

And yet.

Possessions bring no peace. So many wars, so many kingdoms, so much calamity. As I write this, the noncorporate Amazon is burning, and Australia is burning, too. In the north, closer to the places of this poem, icebergs calve into already-brimming seas, and formerly frozen lands reveal the bones and treasures of the dead, melting into mud. COVID-19, a coronavirus, sweeps across the world's population, shifting our understanding of normalcy daily, if not hourly. Rulers stand shaking their fists and shouting, and though the shouting is done these days on Twitter, the content is the same as it ever was. *We will come for you. You don't know who God is. You can't have the riches of the world. Everything is ours.*

Though *Beowulf* is written from the corner of the people in power, we can see the impoverished and imperiled in the exposition. The farmers looking up, fearing the blast, as a dragon scars their fields. The commoners who live abutting the mere, who watch Grendel and his mother and report to their king. The slave who steals a goblet from a dragon, hoping to use it to pay off some unwritten debt to his master. Those who report in this poem often report because they're hoping desperately to change their status, to come in from the cold to a position nearer the fire. And on the other side of it? Kings froth at the mouth and care nothing for their citizens. A hero dies by dragon, and leaves his kingdom to invaders. The home that a soldier or a bride dreams of returning to, when the war is finally over, may be a scorch mark on the earth when they finally make it back.

Storytellers spit a lot of truth in *Beowulf*. They bear dire reports, recaps, and comparisons, or as the Geatish woman does, lament horrors to come. They're also the ones doing the burying, the last survivors. I can only imagine the living role of the *Beowulf* poet—but the poem itself gives us some intriguing examples of scops declaiming material at odds with celebrations. In an oral tradition, even a king's poet would've needed to flex to get the floor. *Beowulf* itself is a flex by the poet, dazzle-camouflaging early English actuality in an imagined elsewhere of monsters and boar-helms. If nothing else, the history of stories is a history of fantastical versions of what we might be and become.

When I think about *Beowulf* these days, some thirty-five years after I first saw Grendel's mother standing alone with her knife and her rage, I often find myself thinking about Beowulf's barrow. Some think it's just meant to be a monument. Others think the barrow is intended to be a beacon, meant to warn ships of jutting land. My interpretation varies depending on the day, but I tend to think that the stories themselves are the lighthouses.

Sometimes, I picture a map of the world, the kind of map I used to pore over as a child, obsessing over the now-familiar warning: *HIC SUNT DRACONES*. On that imaginary map, I've added story-lighthouses. They're all over the place. *Look here*, their light tells us. *Here's a safe spot to tie up your boat and disembark. Here's a spot to watch out for.* Out here are dragons. Out here are the stories of those dragons, and of those heroes—and more.

There are also stories that haven't yet been reckoned with, stories hidden within the stories we think we know. It takes new readers, writers, and scholars to find them, people whose experiences, identities, and intellects span the full spectrum of humanity, not just a slice of it. That is, in my opinion, the reason to keep analyzing texts like *Beowulf.* We might, if we analyzed our own long-standing stories, use them to translate ourselves into a society in which hero making doesn't require monster killing, border closing, and hoard clinging, but instead requires a more challenging task: taking responsibility for one another.

MDH
New York City
March 3, 2020

BEOWULF

Bro! Tell me we still know how to speak of kings! In the old
   days,
everyone knew what men were: brave, bold, glory-bound. Only
stories now, but I'll sound the Spear-Danes' song, hoarded for
   hungry times.

Their first father was a foundling: Scyld Scefing.
He spent his youth fists up, browbeating every barstool-brother,
bonfiring his enemies. That man began in the waves, a baby in
   a basket,
but he bootstrapped his way into a kingdom, trading loneliness
   for luxury. Whether they thought kneeling necessary or no,
everyone from head to tail of the whale-road bent down:
10 There's a king, there's his crown!
That was a good king.

Later, God sent Scyld a son, a wolf cub,
further proof of manhood. Being God, He knew

3

how the Spear-Danes had suffered, the misery
they'd mangled through, leaderless, long years of loss,
so the Life-lord, that Almighty Big Boss, birthed them
an Earth-shaker. Beow's name kissed legions of lips
by the time he was half-grown, but his own father
was still breathing. We all know a boy can't daddy
20   until his daddy's dead. A smart son gives
gifts to his father's friends in peacetime.
When war woos him, as war will,
he'll need those troops to follow the leader.
Privilege is the way men prime power,
the world over.

Scyld was iron until the end. When he died,
his warriors executed his final orders.
They swaddled their king of rings and did just
as the Dane had demanded, back when mind
30   and meter could merge in his mouth.
They bore him to the harbor, and into the bosom
of a ship, that father they'd followed, that man
they'd adored. She was anchored and eager
to embark, an ice maiden built to bear
the weight of a prince. They laid him
by the mast, packed tight in his treasure-trove,
bright swords, war-weeds, his lap holding a hoard

4

of flood-tithes, each fare-coin placed by a loyal man.

He who pays the piper calls the tune.

40 His shroud shone, ringed in runes, sun-stitched.

I've never heard of any ship so heavy, nor corpse

so rich. Scyld came into the world unfavored;

his men weighted him as well as the strangers had,

who'd once warped him to the waves' weft.

Even ghosts must be fitted to fight.

The war-band flew a golden flag over their main man;

the salt sea saluted him, so too the storms,

and Scyld's soldiers got drunk instead of crying. *me*

They mourned the way men do. No man knows,

50 not me, not you, who hauled Scyld's hoard to shore,

but the poor are plentiful, and somebody got lucky.

Finally, Beow rolled into righteous rule,

daddying for decades after his own daddy died.

At last, though, it was his turn for erasure:

his son, the Halfdane, ran roughshod, smothering

his father's story with his own. He rose in the realm

and became a famous warlord, fighting ferociously

dawn to dusk, fathering his own horde of four,

heirs marching into the world in this order: Heorogar,

60 Hrothgar, Halga, and I heard he hand-clasped his

daughter

(her name's a blur) to Onela. Tender, she rendered that
    battle-Swede
happy in fucking, where before he'd only been happy in fighting.

War was the wife Hroth̶gar wed first. Battles won,
(rodger)
treasures taken. Admirers and kin heard of his fight-fortune,
and flanked him in force. Strong boys grow into stronger men,
and when Hrothgar had an army, his hopes turned to a hall
to home them—a house to espouse his faithful.
More than just a mead-hall, a world's wonder,
eighth of seven. When it was done, he swore,

70 he'd load-lighten, unhand everything he'd won,
worn, and owned, pass to his posse all God's gifts,
save lives and land. He'd keep the kingdom, of course.
He gave far-reaching orders: carpets, carpentry, walls and gables,
tables for seating a clan, rare gifts plated like rare meat,
all for his men. So it rose: a greater hall than any other!
Hrothgar filled it, blood-brother by blood-brother,
and named it Heorot. His words were heard and heralded,
and yes, yes, bro! The man was more than just talk:
he gave good gifts. His war-wedded wore kings' rings,

80 and drank their leader's mead. Nightly, he feted his fight-family
with fortunes. The hall loomed, golden towers antler-tipped; ∧
it was asking for burning, but that hadn't happened yet. _love._
You know how it is: every castle wants invading, and every family
has enemies born within it. Old grudges recrudesce.

6

Speaking of grudges: out there in the dark, one waited.

He listened, holding himself hard to home,

but he'd been lonely too long, brotherless,

sludge-stranded. Now he heard and endured

the din of drinkers. Their poetry poisoned his peace.

90 Every night, turmoil: raucous laughter from Heorot,

howling of harps, squawking of scops.

Men recounting the history of men like them. *] ∨ meta*

The Almighty made Earth for us, they sang.

Sun and moon for our (de)light,

fens full of creatures for our feasting,

meres to quench our thirst.

Heorot's hall-dwellers caroused by candlelight,

stumbling to sleep with the sunrise, replete,

lambs bleating comfort, ease-pleased,

100 until the night wakefulness moved their watcher to wrath.

gvendel

Grendel was the name of this woe-walker,

Unlucky, fucked by Fate. He'd been

living rough for years, ruling the wild:

the mere, the fen, and the fastness,

his kingdom. His creation was cursed

under the line of Cain, the kin-killer.

The Lord, long ago, had taken Abel's side.

Though none of that was Grendel's doing,

he'd descended from bloodstains.
110 From Cain had come a cruel kind,
seen by some as shadow-stalked: monsters,
elves, giants who'd ground against God,
and for that, been banished.

Under a new moon, Grendel set out
to see what horde haunted this hall.
He found the Ring-Danes drunk,
douse-downed, making beds of benches.
They were mead-medicated, untroubled
by pain, their sleep untainted by sorrow.
120 Grendel hurt, and so he hunted. This stranger
taught the Danes about time. He struck, seized
thirty dreaming men, and hied himself home,
bludgeoning his burden as he bounded, for the Danes
had slept sweetly in a world that had woken him,
benefited from bounty, even as they'd broken him.

When golden teeth tasted the sky,
Grendel's silent skill was seen. His kills—
grim crimson spilt on banquet-boards.
The war-horde wailed at the spoiling of their sleep,
130 at the depths they'd dived in darkness, while their enemy ate.
A mournful morning. Their leader sat at his plate, old overnight,

8

impotent at this ingress. The band tracked the invader, but not
   to his lair.
They had prayers to call out, and pains to bear.
Grendel did not stay himself from slaughter. The next night
a second slaying, and then another, his rope played out and
rotted through, a cursed course plotted without mercy,
and corse after corse cold in his keep. Bro, it was easy
after that to count the weepers: men fleeing to cotes
beneath the king's wings. You'd have to have been a fool to miss
140 the malice of the Hell-dweller, now hall-dwelling. Those who
      lived, left—
or locked themselves in ladies' lodgings, far from fault lines.
Those who stayed? Slain.

For twelve snow-seasons, Grendel reigned over evening.
Hrothgar suffered, Heorot buffeted, no hero to hold it.
Every outsider talked shit, telling of legends and losses.
Hrothgar's hall became a morgue, dark marks on
      floorboards.
No songs, no scops, no searing meat, no blazing fire.
And Grendel, incomplete, raided relentlessly.
   Dude, this was what they call a blood feud, a war
150 that tore a hole through the hearts of the Danes.
Grendel was broken, and would not brook peace,
   desist in dealing deaths, or die himself.

He had no use for stealth—he came near-nightly,
and never negotiated. The old counselors knew better
than to expect a settlement in silver from him.
Ringless, Grendel's fingers, kingless,
his country. Be it wizened vizier or beardless boy,
he hunted them across foggy moors, an owl
mist-diving for mice, grist-grinding their tails
160 in his teeth. A hellion's home is anywhere
good men fear to tread; who knows the dread this
marauder mapped?

Grendel, enemy to everyone, waged his war
without an army, lonesome as he lapped
the luxurious lengths of Heorot. He howl-haunted
the hall at night, the gold-gifter's throne throwing
shade at him, his soul burning with dark flame.
He couldn't touch the treasure, or tame
his yearning, for he'd been spurned by God.

170 Times were hard for the prince of the Scyldings, too,
heart-shattered, battered spirit spent.
Men came to advise, bringing pithy plots
and plans to arrest Hrothgar's awful guest.
They bent themselves to idols, and offered up
their own spells, that a soul-slayer might suddenly
show up and save them. That was their nature,

these heathens, hoping at the wrong heavens,
remembering Hell, but nothing else.
They knew no true Lord, no God, no Master.
180 They, too, were cursed, yet thought themselves clear.
Bro, lemme say how fucked they were,
in times of worst woe throwing themselves
on luck rather than on faith, fire-walkers
swearing their feet uncharred, while
smoke-stepping. Why not face
the Boss, and at death seek
salves, not scars?

So it went for years, the Hell-sent raider harrowing
the Halfdane's son, who sat in silence, brooding
190 over unhatched hopes, while in the dark his
people shuddered, salt-scourged by weeping,
by nights spent waking instead of sleeping.

News went global. In Geatland, Hygelac's right-hand man
heard about Grendel. Bro, here was a warrior
like no other: massive, mighty, born of noble
blood. He called for a ship to be readied
for his band, and boasted he'd try his teeth on this tale,
sail in as a savior over the swan-road, seek that king
and lend a hand as defender. His elders
200 understood his quest, and though he was dear to them,

11

they knew better than to spear him with speeches.
They augured the omens—ooh!—and ushered him onward.

He found fourteen fists for hire, the boldest men
of the Geats, and enlisted them as fighters.
He, as their captain, went aboard to pilot
the vessel, with sea-skill, through
keen currents and mean depths.
Soon it was time to depart:
the boat's belly was wet,
210 and beneath the land-locks
these warriors met, cheering,
bringing battle-gear into her bosom. *) again why*
As sand spit and surf sang, they pushed off
and sent themselves to sea, made men.
The wind sent them surging.
With a foam-feathered throat,
their bird flew free, sailing with certainty
over salt waters. On the second day,
she sought a shore, and the men saw cliffs,
220 crags uplifting from the ocean:
the end of the voyage. Overboard
the Geats leapt, shifting from sailors to soldiers,
the moment their soles touched solid earth.
Their weapons rattled as they moored the boat,
their mail unveiled in sunlight.

They thanked God for easy passage
and sweet seas.

Far above them, the Scylding's watchman
waited. It was his duty to keep
230 these cliffs unclimbed. When his gaze hit
gleam: swords and shields glittering
across the gangplank, passing without permission,
Hrothgar's man set out for the sand on horseback,
straight spear in hand, to stand
formally and question them:

"How dare you come to Denmark
costumed for war? Chain mail and swords?!
There's a dress code! You're denied.
I'm the Danes' doorman; this is my lord's door.
240 Who are you that you dare steer your ship
for our shore? I'm the watcher of these waters,
have been for years, and it's my duty to scan the sea
for shield-bearing dangers to Danes. I've never seen
any force come so confidently over swells, certain of welcome,
no welcome won. Did you send word? No! Were you invited?
No! You're not on the guest list. And, also, who's the giant?
What weapons does he hold? Oh, hell no.
He's no small-time hall-soldier, but noble!
Look at his armor! I'm done here!

13

250 Spies, state your secrets, or be denounced.

Who are you, what's your business,

where'd you come from?

I'll ask one more time.

You're not coming past this cliff.

Answer now, or bounce.

You, men: Who? Where? Why?"

Their leader unlocked his word-hoard.

He was the senior soldier, so he spat certainty:

"We are Geats, born and bred, bound

260 to Hygelac. My father was Ecgtheow.

No doubt you've heard of him. He was famous.

He lived through winters that would've

pressed the life from a lesser, and though

he's long since left us, everyone, the world over,

knows my daddy's name. We come in peace,

looking for your lord and land-shield,

the son of the Halfdane. Kindly give us

directions and we'll get gone.

We're here to offer ourselves up

270 to the Dane's lord, and our plans

are open, no secrets from you.

Is it true that something savage

walks at night? We've heard the stories,

that misery stalks and rages here,
that good men are endangered here,
by a stranger in this country.
We come to counsel your king
on how to cleave his reaver,
and court calm. If there's respite
280 to be had, I'm the lad to bring it.
Otherwise, Hrothgar will be grieving
and desperate as long as his
hall hangs—I see it there—
at the horizon."

The watchman was unmoved, his authority innate.
He sat tall on horseback. "I know
the difference between words and deeds,
as anyone with half a brain does.
Thus far, I'll endorse your scheme:
290 you seem a troop true to my lord.
The rest is in the proving.
Come, then, bring your battle-gear.
I'll lead you to my leader,
and send my guards to circle
your new-tarred ship on the sandbar,
until it's time for her to rise ring-prowed
over this rolling road and be boarded again

by whichever of you—if any?—
survive the sword-storm you've sought."

300 Off they went, agreed, leaving
their own mount, that wide wave-rover,
hitched to rope and anchor.
Boars bristled from their cheek-shields,
gold forced into fierce forms by fire.
The watchman led them toward their war.
Fifteen men heeded him and marched
with speed, until the timbered hall
was before them, shimmering, golden,
the structure best known under the sun and stars
310 to every citizen of Earth.
This was a place real men could be rebirthed,
and their guide pointed the path to it,
then turned tail, saying:
"I've been away from my sea-view too long.
May the Father leave you living.
For me, I return to my ocean-post,
to scan the shore for
other enemies."

The road was stone-cobbled, and kept them
320 coming correct, a straight line of marchers,

war-garb gleaming, chains linked by hardened hands,
their armor ringing, loud as any hall-bell. By the time
they arrived in Heorot, dressed for demons,
they were sagging, sea-stung. They stacked shields,
wood-weathered, against the walls, then sat down
on benches, their metal making music. Their spears,
they stood like sleeping soldiers, tall but tilting,
gray ash, a death-grove. Each maker of armor-din
was twinned to his weapon. A man of Hrothgar's
330 company, admiring them, inquired:

"What kingdom sent you here, boys, with your crests
and shields, your gilt helmets and gray-clothed
chests, your sharpened spears? I'm Hrothgar's
herald and officer, and in all my years
I've never seen such an impressive
assembly of outlanders. You've too much style
to be exiles, so I expect you must be
heroes, sent to Hrothgar?"

like outlanders?

The man—we know him, his name means nerve—
340 the leader of the Geats, hard-core in his helmet,
spoke their mission succinctly:
"We're Hygelac's reserve, trained
and ready. Beowulf's my name.

If the Halfdane's son, your leader and lord,
will allow me to come to him,
I'll explain my errand in a few words."

Wulfgar, a Wendel warrior, renowned and warranted
for wisdom and for the tempered edge of his nature,
replied: "I'll ferry your request to our king
350 and ring-giver, Lord of the Scyldings,
and see what, if anything, he offers
in response. I'll return with his answer
as quickly as he
gives it me."

He went with haste to Hrothgar's throne.
The old man was gray, huddled in pain
with his retainers. Bold Wulfgar
stood submissive at his shoulder—he knew the score.
He whispered the matter to his lord:
360 "Geatlanders have come ashore, sea-sullied
from their long sail. Their captain and compeller
is called Beowulf, and he petitions for words
with you. Hrothgar, most generous,
don't deny them. They're well-dressed,
thus well-born, and thus worthy.
And the man who led them here—
he looks so right! His chest, broad in girth,

his armor blazing, bright!
Blatantly of noble birth."

370 Hrothgar, the Scyldings' helm, lifted his head:
"Beowulf? I knew him when he was a boy, and
I knew his daddy, too, Ecgtheow, with whom
Hrethel the Geat bedded his daughter down.
Their son and heir is here to bring health to me!
A crew of mine once crossed to Geatland
with gifts from me to his father, and they
brought back a cargo of stories.
Ecgtheow's boy, they said, had a handgrip
as strong as that of thirty men! As for his band
380 of Geats—hurry, let them in! Holy!
How good is God?! A hero's been sent here
by Heaven to defend the Danes from Grendel!
At least, that's what I hope he's come to do.
If he relieves the pressure on our Paradise,
I'll pay him in gold! Go back before he comes
to his senses and runs. Bid him appear
before his father's friend: he's more than welcome
here in Denmark!"

Wulfgar returned to the Geats, stood at the door,
390 and said: "My king, the East-Danes' leader-in-arms,
tells me he knows your father, and that

you seafarers are welcomed into Heorot. He hails
you, as he would homecoming soldiers. Go, dressed
in your war-gear, your helms, your masks,
and present yourselves to Hrothgar.
No shields necessary, nor spears, boys,
leave your slaughter-slingers here."

Beowulf arose, and around him rose his armored army,
though some stayed to guard the war-hoard, by request.
400 They hastened behind their leader through Heorot's radiance.
Their battle-bringer stood before the fire, glowing,
and considered his words, his chain mail the myth-protecting
work of a smith, links netted to one another
for war-glory. His helmet made him look harder,
so he spoke from beneath it:

"My respects to Hrothgar. I'm a kinsman
of Hygelac, and over the years, no boasts—
I've been known for my promise and prowess.
I heard tell of Grendel from sailors—seriously,
410 the whole world knows the stories, swapped and sworn,
of Heorot Hall's early curfew, how every night
you surrender to silence when the sun sprints
out of Heaven, leaving the celestial dome dark.
Every elder knew I was the man for you, and blessed

my quest, King Hrothgar, because where I'm from?
I'm the strongest and the boldest, and the bravest and the best.
Yes: I mean—I *may* have bathed in the blood of beasts,
netted five foul ogres at once, smashed my way into a troll den
and come out swinging, gone skinny-dipping in a sleeping sea
420 and made sashimi of some sea monsters.

Anyone who fucks with the Geats? Bro, they have to fuck
    with me.
They're asking for it, and I deal them death.
Now, I want to test my mettle on Grendel, best him,
a match from man into meat. Just us two,
hand to hand. *Sweet.* Let me ask one thing, though,
King of the Bright-Danes, Friend of Men, Dire-Defender
Against the Dark, He Who Knows What It Means to Fight—
trust me on this. Don't refuse my humble request.

We came a long way, me and my men, to conquer
430 your curse and cleanse Heorot. This task should be ours
and ours alone, as discussed. I'm told your pest
mocks metal? In that case, I'll make my man
Hygelac proud, his fame fiercer.
Your boy will enshroud his blade, and
fight with fingers and nails.
No sword, no shield, no safety net,
nothing but my grip, a hand-clasped battle
to the death. When we see who wins,

we'll know who's got God's favor.

440 If it's Grendel—I'll be a mere chapter
in his gory story. He'll feast on Geats,
ripping my men limb from limb,
and I won't be there to protect them.
I'll be dead, too, cheekbones chewed
and face forgotten, my body dragged
to his lair, where he'll fare alone on my
severed head, make a banquet of my flesh,
he and I, alone again, naturally. Don't cry
for this broken boy, don't lay out what's left of me.

450 If warfare revokes my pass to Earth's kingdom,
just send this mail-shirt made by Weland—
willed to me by my grandfather Hrethel—to Hygelac.
Horrors happen, I'm grown, I know it.
Bro, Fate can fuck you up."

Hrothgar, the Scyldings' own skull-protector,
had some things to say: "Beowulf, I count you
a favored fight-friend now. Your father?
I knew him from a feud, which he began,
by killing Heatholaf, that, too, hand to hand—

460 and Heatholaf was a Wulfing, so that shit
couldn't stand. Your father's country
wouldn't keep him—they threw him out—

and he set sail over sea to me. I was
a young king of the Danes then, hauling up a hoard
of treasure, that ladder's rungs burnt
beneath me. My brother Heorogar had died,
and he was the firstborn, the better.
I was the lesser brother, but it didn't matter. I fixed
your father's feud with fistfuls of old gold, my treasure
470 shipped to stop his country's wound. Ecgtheow
owed me allegiance ever after.
Oh, it hurts my head that the world knows
of my grief, of Heorot's heartbreaker. Is there
laughter in far-off places, at me, and at my men?
I'm humiliated my hall-force has bent to Grendel's
greed, and I'm short of saviors, bleeding the brave,
feeding them to Fate. God giving ground not to heroes,
but to this twelve-winter shit-season!
And yet, over and over, when golden mead
480 was pouring, warriors swore their safety
was nothing compared to Heorot's.
They'd sleep with swords, with certainty,
but when the sun rose . . . slaughter. Benches
bloody, no sign of those brave soldiers, the floor a pool,
where once it was a playground for poets. It's all
written in red. Know before you dine, Beowulf:
your predecessors are deceased. But sit down, my new old friend.

Boy, enjoy the feast. Take your place in the tale of
my heroes and their hopes."

490 A banquet-bench was brought, an empty one,
so every Geat could sit beside his brothers,
and there they dined, in splendor. At their shoulders
stood a server, and he held a jeweled ewer
filled with mead, sweet for singing and for feasting.
A scop sang, too, his voice surging like a swallow
into the verging arches of Heorot, cheering for this party
of Danes and Geats, all bold men met to bet on Beowulf.

Near Hrothgar's feet squatted Unferth, Ecglaf's son,
unconvinced, whispering churlish words. Beowulf's
   bravado
500 bristled him, and envy ate him alive. He'd historically been
   glorious,
and the notion that another, more notorious under Heaven,
might enjoy greater greatness, made him gnash.

"Bro, do you happen to be the Beowulf
who challenged Breca in the open ocean,
insisting you should swim in shark-seas
for no reason but to prove your petty prowess?
Boasting that no boat should guard your lives,
but that you should risk them recklessly?

I heard no one could convince you two of clarity,
510 that you dove overboard, surfing on stupidity,
swearing you knew the currents better than any other,
and that you, swole as a troll fed on travelers,
were superior to any swell.
You lolled for seven nights in wintry waters,
and in the end? He outswam your fool self,
skipped to shore unscathed though uncertain,
and rolled onto the sand safely, in the land
of the Heotho-Reams. From there, he went
to his home country, where the Brandings
520 adored him, a calm and pleasant place,
and returned to his hall, his host.
His boyish boast was proven, yes, he'd
bested Beowulf. No matter your other battles,
the tales you told, the lines you sold,
buddy, at least you lived. This time?
Bro, know it: no one's ever lasted
a night clasped in Grendel's arms."

Beowulf, Ecgtheow's son, wasn't fazed:
"Well actually, *buddy*, sit down, you're drunk.
530 Unferth, you've run your mouth about Breca, me,
and our sea-swagger, but let me drop some truth
into your tangent. I've been better on the water,
deeper in the drink, and stronger in the swim,

than any man alive. Breca and I were boys

together. Our desires were only dares, one upon

the other, brother to brother, maybe you know this story?

But hold up: I forgot, you've got no brothers left. *boom*

roasted

We declared ourselves adventurers, and so we swam,

swords in hands for safety, unsheathed, father-forged.

540 We knew there were sharks. No one here is stupid.

He couldn't float freer or swim straighter than I,

and I had no urge to leave him or lose the lesser

swimmer. I was Breca's lifeguard. I knew my duty.

The rains rocked us, and storms shook us, and for five nights

we floated, warring against winds from the north,

the waves like blades, bone-cold, until at last,

we were blown apart, the biting beasts of the bottom

roiling up to wring me, wrestling me to the seafloor.

All that held me was my armor, clasped hands

550 made of gold, chain mail gainsaying waves and wet,

the work of ancestors forging my ferocity.

It kept me bold enough to fight when a monster *orca?*

dragged me down and gripped me, ripping at my skin.

I was pinned, swaddled in squalor. Last chance, I took it—

I put that monster down, I made it a sleeper as it leapt,

severed its spine, spiked its skull, and split it into smithereens.

My own strength sank that sea monster, and

soon I was fighting again, lower than any human's sight,

outside even the edges of God's light. Dark deeps, Hell's creatures

560 in them, swinging my sword beneath the eyes of the world.

I would not be eaten, nor beaten, no skewered swimmer I,

no drowned dinner for a circle of cold companions,

gobbling my guts, glutted on my gold.

At dawn, I surfaced in a slurry of scales,

floating flotsam where formerly there'd been fangs.

I'd sacrificed myself to save every subsequent seafarer

from deep despair, and the monsters

of the dark were gone. The east was gilded

with God, and the sea was smooth.

570 I could see the shore, the strong cliffs rising,

built of their own bruises. If a man's brave enough,

Fate, when on the fence, will often spare him.

I'd never brag, but the truth is, my sword slew

nine singular scavengers that night. There are

no oceangoing stories more awful

than mine, no tales of greater terror,

no other man so sea-stalked, but I survived,

my salvation in my own hands. The waves

bore me shoreward, attending me, and left me

580 at long last in the land of the Finns. The End.

I've racked my brain, bro, but, Unferth,

I can't unpack any similar stories of

heroics from you. Let me say it straight:

You don't rate and neither did Breca

when it came to battle. The gulf? You're cattle,

and I'm a wolf. I'm not even mentioning your sins,
your kin-killing, your brother-beating:
I'm not the man to damn you.
No shit, though, Unferth, if you were
590 the bitter-brawling brave you claim to be,
your king wouldn't have suffered a single night
of Grendel's rampage, no bitten bones,
no hall-horror, no chaos in his kingdom.
Grendel was aware he had nothing to fear here.
Your sword's soft, son. No warrior
awaited him in Heorot. The Scyldings
were unshielded, their hall unguarded. He knew
he could crush you, comfort himself with grappling,
grind your bones to make his bread. He's got no fear
600 of beer-hall brothers, but, this you can quote—he'll fear me.
There're no guns of note on anyone but me and my Geats.
Come on, Ecglaf's son. Beat me. Or better yet, make me a bet
that Grendel's maker won't be met. Then, if you brave boys
feel like drinking, I'll serve you ale for breakfast, the sun shining
on silver and gold, daylight yours, after night's been mine."

This speech was more than enough to convince the ring-giver,
his hair gray, his war-grace blazing. The king
of the Bright-Danes knew now he could defend his people
with an assist from this warrior of the wider world.

610 He got the party started, loud and lordly,
and the hall welled up and overran with laughter.

Wealhtheow appeared among them then, Hrothgar's queen.
Gleaming, her gown golden, she chose her chance to charm.
She was the cup-keeper. She raised it high to show the men,
then bore it to Hrothgar, Dane's delight,
her husband and home-holder. She held it to his lips
and he drank deeply, the love of country in each draft.
He threw it back as fast as once he'd drawn his sword,
this old, old lord of war, and his men cheered. She went round,

620 a Helming-hostess, treading with purpose, rings shining,
beer-sounding soldiers, old and young, both of her own
    house
and the sea-slayers', goblet held to her breast. Hashtag: blessed.
At last, Beowulf was before her, fingers outstretched.
She welcomed him carefully to Heorot as a hero,
a man who'd answer hopes with hands, and who might,
please God, finally redeem her land from Hell.

The warrior took the cup from Wealhtheow, eager
for the end of festivities, for the night and fight to come.
He was ready for his war, and a wight awaited him.

630 Beowulf sipped, and the son of Ecgtheow assured the queen:
"Woman, I knew my plan when I set off for this coast.

29

Before I put my band in that boat, already I was bent
on victory. I mean to give you a show, to make
your sleep safe or be slain myself, Grendel's spikes
in my skin. I'm gonna do as real men do,
and render myself a reaper, bleed him dry,
or let Death attend me and cup-bear in your place,
here in this mead-hall."

The hostess was impressed by Beowulf's boasts.
640 Brass balls, if nothing else. She posted up
beside Hrothgar, queenly, her gold glinting.

There was more celebration, the kind of party
that hadn't been heard of in a while,
rowdy and riotous, loud with laughter
and proud poetry, until the Halfdane's heir
arrested rhyme for rest. The fiend, he knew,
had been silent, subterranean while the sun shone,
but now it was night. Darkness draped the Earth.
The happy hall would soon be a demon's domain,
650 the men his dreadful diet. Shadows slunk from the swamp,
and mists mossed the cliffs and hillsides. The men stood
witness as their leaders took leave.

Hrothgar wished luck on the late-lingerer,
gave him all hall-power, and proclaimed:

"I've never, not in all my years of shield-bearing,
trusted any other could hold this hall from horrors.
It's yours tonight. May you ward it well:
it was built for the tenders of the flame. Keep
your reputation in mind, and stand unyielding
660 against the brute. If I find you alive in the morning,
I'll reward you beyond your wildest dreams."

Hrothgar and his household left the hall,
the leader and protector of the Scyldings
bound to Wealhtheow's bed for comforts—
his wifely strife-soother. The king, it would
prove, had appointed a watcher whose muscles
were monster-matched, Fate-directed
to the Dane-chief as a prince-protector.
The Geats knew all this already. They trusted
670 their man, his iron arms and brawling brand.
Beowulf stripped, removed his breastplate and helmet,
handed off his fine-forged heirloom sword—
his servant swooned over that sweet smith's steel,
ordered in no uncertain terms to ward and keep it safe.

Beowulf headed to bed, swollen with certainty,
and swore, this mortal gift from God:
"I don't know what you've heard about hand to hand,
but my hands are better than good, man. I'm direr

31

than any demon. I won't slice Grendel with a sword, boys—
680 too simple—I'd end him too quickly; it'd be unfair.
He has no skill, only reptilian skin. His mind's
got no flair for strategy, though his strength
is savant. Nope, I'll go unarmed into this evening,
and he'll take it on the chin—if he's got guts
enough not to flee. May God referee
this ring, and declare the winner whichever
of us he wishes."

Then Beowulf dropped his head to pillow,
and beside him rested his command of brave men,
690 warriors of sea and sleep. They were ready
to see life's end, and didn't expect to lay eyes
on their heartland again, not familiar soil,
not their parents, not their wives. They knew
the story of the slaughterer, the dozen years Danes
had been driven from their home-hall. The Almighty, though,
had other plans, a tapestry of terror threaded with triumph,
the Weather-Geats the victors. They'd rise with their leader,
crush the challenger, and cruise through creation
kinsmen to a king. You know how it goes:
700 God's the final decider, and men only the
question-askers, students seeking solace.

In the dead of night, Grendel emerged,
a predator without need of torch,
serged to the shadows. Nearly all the guards
were sleep-sagging, chins to chests. They'd stitched
themselves to God, and knew no enemy could hem
them in, not without Almighty approval.
Just one thane waited, feigning sleep
as the hour grew late. He lay awake, on high alert.

710 Hidden by fog, Grendel roved the moors, God-cursed,
grudge worsening. He knew who he hunted:
wine-drunk, mead-met men, and he pined
for his prey. Under storm clouds, he stalked them,
in his usual anguish, feeling a forbidden hearth,
that gilded hall atop the hill, gleaming still,
through years of bloodshed. This was not
the first time he'd hunted in Hrothgar's hall,
but never before nor later had he such hard luck.
No one worthy had historically lain in wait.

720 The warrior worked his way toward the war,
his head and heart hurting, and arrived
at the iron-crossed door. Its hinges howled a welcome,
and his rage ratcheted up. He flung the hatch
wide and leapt into the mead-room, over
decorated floors, into the hold, fury frothing.

His heart crowed as he counted them, man by man,
nested together, roosting like roasting chickens.
He'd be the sort of fox that stalks the night.
Eat his fill, no coo remaining, no bill—only feathers,
730   loose on the floor. Before sunrise, he planned to prise souls
from skeletons. His wyrd, though, would no longer be writ
in others' blood, red footprints to the door and out,
the moors, the mere. No. Tonight was the night
Grendel's goose would be cooked, his funeral
banquet bruised and blue.

Fervid and flexing, faking sleep,
Hygelac's servant spied from his bench,
scanning slit-eyed the long-haunted hall, awaiting
the hunted hunter. At last his enemy struck,
740   snatching a sleeper, sucking him bone-dry,
staining the pale planks red, grunting, gobbling,
gnawing him limb from limb, here a throat,
here a head, fingers, feet—dead.

Hands outstretched to slaughter a second,
Grendel dropped his first course,
spotting the bed where Beowulf slept.
He gripped *that* sleeper, though, and found himself
conscripted, his own hand grabbed
by a commanding Geat. The grasp began

750   the tear that would take Grendel out, rendering him

a revenant in the hall he'd always reveled in.

His bones cracked, but he could not wrestle free

from the clasp, war-wedded to a woe-bringer,

who clung like no human ever clung,

keeping him close. Grendel was an unwilling draftee,

never bested before, nor held hostage.

Now Hygelac's man, chanting the boasts

he'd made his bed-rhyme, climbed from the covers

to get a better grip. Knuckles buckled, joints

760   unjoined. The attacker became the attacked—

racked with pain, attempting to escape,

to race from hall to fens, his hidden highways.

His own grasp unlatched, his flesh-locks loosened,

try though he might to divest himself of Heorot

and return home, dive into the dark and abide

with any awful thing there, stay in stealthy-health

the rest of his days. The room shook, benches splintered,

and Danes dreamt of doom, or quivered, questioning.

The warriors wrestled, muscles bulging, and raged,

770   screaming for their lives, and the hall trembled

but stayed standing, its design fit for fighting,

the wooden walls crossed with iron bands,

a forest fettered together—though from what I've heard,

the mead-benches stood on end and shattered,

gold sigils no match for battle.

The two fighters fought on in the rubble.
I mean, damn, man, until this night, no Scylding
would've believed the hall could be felled
by anything but flame, its ivory and iron,
780 its careful cantilevers. Tonight, though,
it risked timbering.

A wailing clamor rose again, echoing
over the confines, and the North-Danes listened
to the sound of doom's hammer, instability
building a home in the hearts of those who heard it.
The whole hill quaked with the shriek
of that Almighty-abrogate, the loner's lament,
handcuffed by hopelessness, losing to an unforeseen
leader. The warrior holding him was stronger
790 than any monster, more muscular than any man.

That stalwartest of soldiers had no wish
to imprison the invader, only to slay him.
Grendel's life wasn't worth living, and Beowulf
had decided to end it. His own men
stood to as the unarmed enemies swung
heirloom blades willy-nilly;
though, really, their captain needed no safekeeping.
They swung for the slayer's soul, but their struggle
was for naught. They could've stayed sleeping

36

rather than fought, or merely watched
the battle, for their swords, sharp as they were,
couldn't injure the fiend—his spells warded him,
annealing his skin. Still, his death would be agony.
The world clung to his fingers, and life-leaving
wouldn't be swift, no existence-snuffing
instantaneous gift, but sickly slow suffering,
his sinning spirit sent to sink
slowly down to Hell.

He knew it now, he who'd spent seasons haunting
810 this hall, preying on poets, bringing pain to the privileged,
infuriating the Almighty: his body was breached;
its bones were breaking. Hygelac's kinsman had him,
hand-welded. Each of them, living, canceled out the other,
as Cain had Abel, brother unbrothered.
Grendel's shoulder split, tendons twisting,
arteries unscrolled, his limb worried from him,
bested by fatal fists. Beowulf, the winner;
Grendel, dismissed. He ran then, for his grave,
still living. He rushed to the water,
820 wound weeping, lair his last longing.
His hourglass was emptying now,
his days done, and he knew it.
Each heartbeat wrote its number in red,
and the Ring-Danes were delivered

finish
him

of their wretch with a wring:
this enemy was dead.

The ranger had arranged a cleansing, swept the hall
while the Danes were sleeping, done the danger in.
He was pleased with himself, a Geat-son's boasts
830   proven in the Danes' den. He'd unharrowed Heorot Hall,
and Hrothgar's humiliations held no further horrors,
the darkness of recent fate now taking the form
of someone lately late—even if the whole wasn't here,
but only a hand, Grendel's arm, torn off by the hero
at the shoulder and hung on high,
the span of his grasp displayed.

grendel is killed

Bro, I've heard when dawn broke, soldiers
stampeded to the ring-hall, chieftains coming to
contemplate the cooling corpse-portion,
840   warriors and wild men from all over the realm,
wide-eyed with wonder, overwhelmed at the sight
of Grendel's tracks in the dirt, no sorrow there
for those who'd suffered him, but satisfaction at the marks
of misery where he'd conveyed himself from hall door
to mere shore, bleeding out. He'd left a river of gore,
and the warriors had no regrets, imagining him
dropping, a doomed carcass, into those wicked waters,
which even now were blood-clotted, scarlet drifts.

O, the gift of this! That devil-diver, deep in the dark,
850 dimmer, and dimmer yet, dying, dying, dead!
Here was the truth, everyone knew it,
Grendel was headed down, Hell-bent.

Off they went, the elderly officers,
and the young men behind them,
all mounted, white men on white horses,
praising their Heaven-sent hero, Beowulf,
with every word they spoke. Not north, nor south,   *on their*
nor anywhere, they said, was there a man more   *way*
qualified to be king. There was a lot of country
860 between the coasts, a lot of open air beneath the sky,   *back?*
and even there, nope, no one better to rule. Of course,
this unfettered praise wasn't meant to blame Hrothgar
for anything—no, no, that was a good king.
They were giddy enough to gallop for
the first time in years, pale horses racing
on trails long unused, though famous
once for being smooth. And a poet,
a long-term comrade of the king,
a man mindful of meter with a
870 memory made of myriad myths, *nrrfa*
began to compose (*The Tale of Beowulf*:)
his enviable exploits, and Geatish feats,
the sentences rhyming rapturously,

since now the man was elite enough for permanence.
The scop had opinions, and he shared them:
compare/contrast. Stories he'd heard
about another warrior, Sigemund. Verses detailing
that man's hidden past, stealthy acts, dark secrets
spat only into his kinsman's ear. The world-roaming
880 of Wael's defiant heir, all those old tales
whispered to Fitela, from uncle to nephew,
who'd together slain giants, their swords
strong as their certainties.

new char?

"After he died, Sigemund was shaped
into story-glory for his crowning kill,
cutting through the hide of a hoard-holder,
a dragon whose cave he'd crawled inside,
outrageously alone, without even Fitela.
He was fortunate in his fortune-hunting:
890 his sword stabbed the serpent, and sliced it
like butter, straight through scale to stone,
and the dragon died, leaving bounty
and bones to Wael's son, who claimed
the treasure for himself. He loaded his ship
with glitter. The dragon, even dead,
was so embittered it melted, smelting
dark intention into the metal.

"These days, everyone knows Sigemund's name:
the most famous exile. Far and wide
900 he swung his sword, and his fortunes swelled
in the years after King Heremod lost his way.
That king was attacked and betrayed,
stung in Jutland, ultimately undone.
His mood swings had mauled his men,
emboldened his foes, and fractured
his friends. Senility was suspected,
and his advisers sorrowed,
those who'd relied on him to think
clearly, those who'd trusted the inheritor
910 of the throne to behave as his daddy had:
reigning righteously, paying promptly,
shielding the Scyldings' safety.
Beowulf is surely such a man, adored by friends
and men and every living thing, but other kings
have hoarded horrors in their hearts . . ."

While the scop spun, Danes and Geats raced,
harrowing the highway with hooves. The sunlight
was bright and brighter, and young men herded
themselves to Heorot, to gape at the gory
920 glory therein. The king himself, hoary, hallowed

41

hoard-holder, ring-bringer, came boldly from
out of the women's wing, good man incarnate,
flanked by ranks of ladies, his queen beside him,
and paced a path from maid-hall to mead-hall.

Hrothgar stood on the stairs, staring at the ceiling
he'd commissioned. Amid gold and gleam hung
Grendel's attrition, a lacerated limb.

"First and most fervent, we give thanks
to the ever-bearer for this sight, our long struggle
930 cleared in a single night. We've suffered years
of hall-harvesting here, but hard times are done
at last. God is good. Grendel is gone. Only yesterday,
I thought my heart would never be mended,
the evening-rending endless, this house
of heroes red-rouged, my council risking
life and limb to bed down in their home-hall,
and defend this place from demons,
yet every morning, dozens dead.
Now, with an Almighty assist, this man
940 has done what no man did before.
His mother, I forget who she is—is she still alive?—
should be proud of her prince, an answer to prayers.
Beowulf, regardless of whether your parents
survive, you're my son now, adoption won

by wily work. 'Be good to me; I'll be good to you,'
I always say. You'll need nothing in life, boy,
I'll feed you, fete you, and count you
as my foundling. You're a king-to-be.
I've decorated countless others, treated lesser
950 warriors as brothers, and rewarded the inferior
for fearlessness, or what passed for it then.
Now, though, my standards have shifted.
You're more than a man, but an immortal:
your valor in this hall will live in legend.
I implore the Lord to keep you, my ward,
in His grace, and wield His power on your behalf."

Beowulf, Ecgtheow's son, replied:
"We're lucky to be living, having gone into battle
with only bright intentions, against a stranger
960 whose might we hadn't measured. I wish
you'd been awake to watch me bring war to your enemy,
to see him beaten, but it was not to be.
I meant to put him in a headlock, lash him
to his deathbed, and bludgeon him, clench my fists
around his throat, strangle till he gasped his last,
but alas, the Lord set him free.
What can I say? He slithered from my fingers
like a serpent, and slipped my knots, screeching
for the exit. He paid his passage in pulses,

43

970 though, and left a limb behind, holding the door:
his hand, arm, and shoulder. There they stayed,
proof of his incursion, much as he regretted it.
Behold! Nothing could live limited like that.
The last of his blood must have boiled by now,
braiding itself about his body, chaining him
in coils of pain. He's dying now,
if not already dead, a sinner
awaiting sentence. God, not me,
will judge him."

980 Previously prone to calling bullshit,
Unferth, Ecglaf's son, was stymied
as the roomful of nobles took note
of the horrible hand, hanging whole,
armpit to fingertips, high in the eaves.
The nails were notorious, hard as though
smith-forged, and the heathen's hand
was callused as a carpenter's, weathered
by work and warring. Everyone swore
to what they'd seen: no sword could stab
990 through that skin, no fight-fang tear it.

Then all hands were hauled on deck
by order of the king, to restore Heorot to its
former splendor, citizens resurrecting

glamour blunted by gore. The golden threads
in tapestries, depicting scenes of sweeter times,
distractions in gleaming designs, now
hung haphazard in the ruined room.
Reinforced as the walls had been,
they were still wreckage, door hinges bent,
1000 braces broken. Only the ceiling remained uncracked.
The intruder had fled first, afraid of expiring
far from home. Death, no matter our desires,
can't be distracted. We know this much is true,
and it's true for all souls: each of us will one day
find the feast finished and, fattened or famished,
step slowly backward into their own dark hall
for that final night of sleep.

→ New guy?!

In due time, the Halfdane's heir appeared.
Tonight the king would dine triumphant
1010 at his own table, reclaimed from ruin.
Never before had everyone shown up
so festive, so fiery, to pay tribute   beowulf?
to their bounty-bringer. Every major man
was there, pounding cups of mead. Even the king
shouted for rounds, his nephew Hrothulf   ← do we know him?
there beside him, spirits flowing, hearts glowing
in Heorot Hall. Back then, remember,
the Scyldings were not yet inclined

toward treachery, though things would change.

1020 Hrothgar gave his own father's sword to Beowulf,
presented it formally. With it a helmet, mail-shirt,
and war-banner, all precious property of his people.
Beowulf drank deeply, pleased and petted,
feted to the utmost, gifts raining down
upon him like pennies from Heaven.
The Halfdane's sword, the gold, the glitz:
the rest of the hall-soldiers watched it happen.

I mean, personally? I've never seen anything
like it, so many treasures sliding down the table,
1030 a battle-dowry moved from man to man, over ale,
no less. No fighting? No fury? Nope, bro, this was
a certain type of night. The golden helmet, for example,
was ringed with ridges, wrapped in wire to tire any sword
that sought the skull of a shield-warrior occupied
with other enemies. Now the king called for eight
steeds to be led into the hall, each in its own
horse-helmet, harnessed in gold, and one mare
was buckled under Hrothgar's own saddle,
the same saddle he used for swordplay,
1040 gem-dripping, blinged-out, brought forth only
when the king himself was slaying. That man, remember,
was the first to fight in wartime, the first to kill,
swinging before any of his boys could be slain.

46

Ing's descendant dropped all these delights upon Beowulf,
the weapons, the horses, ordering him to use them in health.
Yeah, the lord of Heorot paid properly,
tendered treasure for services rendered in blood.
Anyone knows how fair it was:
bro, more than fair.

1050 And more than this, even, the king bequeathed
to each of the sea-soldiers on Beowulf's bench.
Every life-risker got a golden gift of his own,
and the man who'd been assassinated
by Grendel was vindicated in treasure.
The invader would've murdered many more,
had God not gotten in the mix.
One man's mettle kept the rest
from massacre. You have to look at it
this way, and reconcile yourself:
1060 God's in charge, always has been,
always will be, and anyone who lives long
will endure both ecstasy and ugliness.

It was an hour for singing then, and instruments
were hauled out for the battle-bringing king,
who called for harps, epics, and heroic histories.
Healgamen, Hrothgar's poet, was ready with rhymes,
spitting the saga of the sons of Finn, word-whipping

47

his way into the fight in Friesland, the day
the Danish king, Hnæf of the Scyldings,
1070 fell to lack of fealty.

WHO IS THIS???

"Hildeburh had nothing tender to say
about the Jutes and their loyalties.
She'd surrendered son and brother here,
her home-hall become a brutal battlefield.
Innocent of crime, yet cursed, captured,
speared, worse. Hoc's daughter was savaged
by sorrow, grief-gutted. Who wouldn't weep,
as dawn drove feud-daggers deeper, the sun scoring
her son's wounds, day breaking upon her dearest dead?
1080 They'd been her heart, her happiness, her hopes.
War had wrung them ragged, dragged them to death
across a court of sword-crossed kin.

"There was no fighting now, no. Finn had only lack left.
He could not attack from here and battle to the end
with Hengest. Though this had been his own hall,
most of his men were dead, and what could Finn,
the host, do to preserve the rest
from their enemies? A truce was his only option,
a partitioned hall, sword split in half,
1090 the Danes quartered in one portion, the Frisian throne
and edifice now a shared territory. Daily, he'd give gifts

to both sides, his hands open as widely
to Hengest and his men, unwillingly ruled over
by their ring-lord's reaper, as to his own men, the Frisians.
They'd all be encouraged in encomiums,
given hope with heirlooms. Everyone would be hostage
to hall-jollity, and beer would be drunk without jeering,
both sides pacified by precious things.
This, then, was the treaty. The agreement
was sealed in gold, all former fighters
guaranteed greed-grace. It was sworn solemnly
to Hengest by Finn, and any Frisian who broke it,
who thought he might divide the room
with whispered insults, raising recent wrath
with snide ribbing, would be pricked.
The sword's point would decide.

"The pyre was built, gold unhoarded, to properly mourn
the Scyldings' king, who slumbered on his death-weald,
awaiting warmth he'd never feel. The landscape was littered
with reddened metal, mail-coats gored, links bent,
boar-shaped helmets, dented where swords had scraped
skulls. Other bodies, too, of noble Danes, unraveled
by gaping wounds, traveling to journey's end.

"Hildeburh sent her son to his last station
at Hnæf's shoulder, their soul-vessels

to be burnt together: family, finally, in flame.
She raised her voice in mourning, keening for her kin
as the pyre was lit. Smoke smothered her song, darkness
made of skin and bone. These men who'd been tended
1120 by those who loved them were carcasses now,
heads melted, wounds running, reopened
for flame-ravens. Fire comes from the same
family as famine. It can feast, unfulfilled, forever.
The dead of both nations were done,
glory days gone for good. The fighters fell away,
finding families and forts across Friesland,
visiting the living, too long close-quartered
with corpses.

"Hengest, though, boarded a wicked winter
1130 in Finn's hall, heart howling for his
own king and hearth, the weather too wild
to loosen his ship. For him, the ice and snow
were tinted red, and kept him clinging
to a killing country. At last, as always happens,
the season shifted to spring. Another year appeared,
sunlight, green tendrils, the earth's bosom in bloom,
a time for returning, the exiled yearning for home . . .
But more than that, to get it done with, the avenging,
without which Hengest would be unmanned.
1140 He itched to bring justice to Jutes.

"When Hunlafing lay a legendary sword in his lap, well—
it was named Flame-Fang for a reason. Any season
is a season for blood, if you look at it in the right light.
The Jutes knew this blade already. They should've
expected it to twist, to key their kingdom.
Hengest only did what he had to do: tipped the pitchers,
spilt the ale, red rivers running under wooden benches.
Finn fell when Guthlaf and Oslaf,
hard henchmen, brought up the last winter's battle,
1150   blaming brutality on their bold host, and their grief
on him, too, the pain of their loss unquenched,
the only remedy blood-balm. The Scyldings washed the walls
with rancor, slew Finn and all his men, and bore away
his world-queen. They ransacked the hall for a hoard,
grabbing all the treasure they could hold, golden collars,
jewels. Onward, then, over the sea, and back to Denmark,
they brought their woman, straight-spined, returning her
to the country she'd come from."

That dark entertainment was done—words had won over wine
1160   long enough. Now laughter conquered conversation.
Serving boys poured pleasure from pitchers. Wealhtheow,
weighted in gold, processed to her place between two good men,
Hrothgar and his nephew Hrothulf, who back then yet trusted
in the links of lineage. There, too, waited Unferth, at the feet

of those men, the Scylding's lords, who trusted him, too—
perhaps not as much as they trusted themselves—
but still, a brave man, though a sibling-slayer,
brilliant, though a brother-breaker.

The lady offered up all she had to trade:

Allusion! ooooo

1170 "Accept this cup from me, my lord of rings, and lift
this golden goblet. Give the Geats their due. Be good
to them who've been good to you. Gifts are for granting,
and your hands should be open, your heart happy,
even as you remember—I know you do—the good men
who gave kith-gifts to you. Heorot's red walls have been
whitewashed, purged of horror. And I hear you've chosen
a brand-new son, this Cain-cleansing warrior. I know you know
that life is short, that you are mortal—the blessings you bask in
today are boons for bequeathing. I ask only that you gift
    the kingdom
1180 to your kin, before your sword is sheathed in smoke. I know
your nephew Hrothulf well, his noble blood, his moral code—
he'll serve our sons and raise them right.
I trust he'll treat them sweetly, if you should die
before he does, repaying our kindness with son-safety.
We took him in when his father died, and if he recalls it at all,
he knows how to behave: we gave the orphan everything,
made him one of our brave men, when he'd have been alone."

She bent then to her boys' bench, where
Hrethric and Hrothmund sat, with all the young sons
1190 of chieftains. There, too, was a grown man, good, great
Beowulf the Geat, positioned between them.

She brought him the cup. She called him friend.
She gave him gold. Her will was wrought
in rings. She offered armlets, garments, a neck-ring:
a collar larger than any I've ever seen,
heavy as Heaven is light, and all of it brighter
and better than any hoard since Hama's,
who himself hooked the flaming throat-chain
of the Brisings, those amber god-reins,
1200 and trekked it back to his own fortress,
fleeing Eormenric's treachery
and securing his soul with gold-barter.

And later, hear it: Hygelac the Geat, Swerting's nephew,
would be the final owner. In his last battle,
beneath banners, he'd hold to his hoard, fighting furiously,
shackled to this sparkling string, this precious, poisonous
    thing.
Fate would fell him and his prideful priorities, the Frisians
following his feud-fuel, and he in heavy armor, gem-governed,

would be slain. He'd worn that same sparkle when he crossed

1210 the sea-coupe, but even champagne goes flat. His bling
would go to Frankish kings, from plundered breastplate
to that famous throat-chain, and lowlier warriors
would gloat over the goners, getting what gold they could
from Geat corpses, a field full of the forgotten.

The hall thundered with handclaps. Wealhtheow went on
with her gift-giving, thus witnessed: "Take this golden collar,
dear Beowulf. May it keep your head on straight.
Wear this mail-shirt, too—a treasure of my people.
May it protect your heart-hoard. Guide my two sons,

1220 guard them, keep them as they are tonight,
and I will keep you as *you* are: draped in delights.
You're famous here, and long after your lifetime,
you'll be known, your story sweeping as the sea,
shores borne into being by waves of words.
My prince, may you be blessed by this bounty.
Keep my sons close. Treat them as we treat one another
here in Heorot: tenderly, trustingly, loyally.
No one conspires to hurt—only to hold fast with brothers.
Believe me, Beowulf: my thanes' wishes align with mine.

1230 The sole desire of those drinking here,
is to do my bidding when it comes to you."

She settled into her seat. Wine waterfalled into men's mouths—
it was a banquet unmatched in munificence. After all,
they had no foretelling of Fate's fixed plans. A shadow
stretched over sweetness, formless and fatal.
Night fell and Hrothgar readied himself for rest,
his quarters calling him to sleep. Men stood guard,
as they always had. The floor that bristled with benches
became a swan-road, white waves of bolster and feathers,
1240 and though one of those drinkers turned dreamers
was doomed, he didn't know it.

The Geat's shields served as shining headboards,
and on each bench was arranged a helmet, hulking,
a mail-shirt with rings like linked fingers, and
a splinterless spear, tree-sleek, ready for wrath
anytime, to be brought into play without notice,
as was the habit of their homeland and war-wanderings.
They were ready to wreak havoc, anytime, anyplace—
their lord was a lucky lord. The Geats were hard-core,
1250 but even Geats need sleep, so sleep swept them away.
One dreamer would die dreaming. This was nothing new,
given Grendel's former residence in the golden hall,
but his eviction had made evil dwindle in the minds
of the defenders. That story, they thought, was over.

There was another chapter. An avenger lay in wait,
counting sworded seconds until the latest hour,
her heart full of hatred. Grendel's mother,
warrior-woman, outlaw, meditated on misery.
She lived, ill-fated, sinking beneath cold currents
1260   to her kingdom under-country, her line linked
to extinction since Cain crossed swords with Abel
and fled, murder-marked, to make his home
in wastelands, solitary and silent. From Cain came
more misery, a legacy of lost souls.
Grendel was one of those, banished and blasted.
He'd found a waker among the dreamers, a battle
amid the beds, and wrestled the warrior who'd
woken into war. Beowulf saw himself as God's gift,
Grendel as a goner; he used his strength to slay
1270   the intruder, trusting in his Father to protect him,
as He always had. He bled the hellion, and
Grendel fled piecemeal, no Heaven for him,
no honey, only rushing through a haunted hall to die
in his own mausoleum. Now his mother was here,
carried on a wave of wrath, crazed with sorrow,
looking for someone to slay, someone to pay in pain
for her heart's loss. She found the path,
and made her way to Heorot.

Ring-Danes were dreaming there, a murdering herd
1280 of sleepers, drooling, drunk, their feast filling them.
They were the cream of the crop, but soon
they'd be chaff, scythed from swordsmen
into skeletons. She was the one to do it.
The horror wasn't muted by the measure
of women's strength against men's brawn.
Both can hold slaying swords, glazed with gore,
and score the boar-crests from war-helmets,
warming them with blood.

In Heorot Hall, hard-honed blades were yanked
1290 from over benches, shields shouldered
to cover blinking sleepers, waking bareheaded,
barechested, stunned by her arrival. She moved
swiftly, knowing she had only moments to sift men
for her vengeance and remain among the living.
She tore a warrior from his bed, and dragged him,
defenseless, to her fen. This was Hrothgar's best friend,
most adored on the land between the two salt seas,
warrior and retainer. She slew him sleeping.

Beowulf was lucky, bedded elsewhere. After the brawl,
1300 gift-quarters had been appointed him like rings.
The Geat was asleep when Grendel's mother struck.
Heorot Hall howled—she'd taken their trophy, too:

Grendel's hand! Man by man, they squalled.
This was unjust, a bad bargain that both sides should suffer
losses, though the war was dealt and done, themselves
the clear winners. The wise king, gray and battle-brittle,
moaned when he knew the news, that his closest adviser,
nearest-to-ear, was no more, doornail-dead.

Beowulf, blood-blessed boy, was hauled from sleep,
1310 hustled hungover to the king's bedside.
Boot to boot with his band,
he marched to the room where
Hrothgar waited, grim and gloomy,
wondering if his fate was fucked forever,
the Almighty refusing to relent.
Beowulf and his boys threw the doors open
to sunlight and rattled the floorboards,
no ground given to grief. Beowulf thundered
up to the morose prince and asked:
1320 Had Hrothgar slept well?

Hrothgar had no words. He said some anyway.
"Don't speak to me of happiness! Hard times
have come again! The Danes are in darkness!
Æschere is murdered! Yrmenlaf's big brother,
and my best friend! My battle bro when ranks
were closing and boar-helms bashed

into brainpans! He was there, hand to my heart,
a man like no other, terror-tested, never bested
until tonight, when a slaughterer withdrew him,
1330 and spirited him from Heorot!
Where is she? Who knows!
Glutting on gobbets, after murdering him
unopposed. This is on *you*. She threw
herself into a blood feud after you slew her son
Grendel last night, tore him and bore him
into the afterlife, never mind years of his own crimes.
You gripped him, held him, and he lost the fight,
fell to the mat, and died. He's followed by another now,
an evil intruder, his mother, fueled by fury, a woman
1340 seeking vengeance for her son. She goes too far,
even as a soldier might in avenging his king,
grieving the loss of his ring-giver.
That hand, which once stretched wide, filled
with golden gifts, now still and cold.

"Well. I've heard my people, those simple citizens
who live out in the muddy country, say they've seen
these two together, roaming the moor,
wading the mere, heath-rambling and of a height.
One is, as far as they can tell, a woman,
1350 and the other, misshapen, formed like a man,
but larger than any man has a right to be.

He was named Grendel, a fatherless son.

Who knows whether he had other kin.

He was a sin-walker, is all they said,

those who've talked to me of these things.

They say the two stalked the hillsides,

the concealed country. They denned with wolves

and dove in windy rivers, slipped like mist-fish

into the fen and through it, down into the

1360 darkest places underwater and underground,

cliff-bound. It's not far from here, the mere,

but it's a world away, a forest frosted

even in green months, old wood, wicked

and well-rooted. Water reflects trees

like tangled teeth, a gaping maw that, at night,

is lit with flames in the flood. No one's ever

touched the bottom. No one born of man, anyway.

Men can't go in. Even animals, a heath-hopping hart,

held to mere's edge by hounds, would sooner spin

1370 on hooves and fight, lower horns, and ready itself for death

than step upon that stinking sod and dive into the dark.

That is a bad place. Waves roil, and taste the sky's edge,

winds gust, clouds spit and spark, and when it storms,

mere mixes with mist, geysers up, and Heaven moans.

I'll say it again: this is on you.

Everything depends on a boy who knows nothing of this terror,

not least what you might fear when you get there,

the nerves that might make you quake
in horror's homestead. Go in, if you dare.
1380 I'll pay in gold, old and new, heirlooms
and holdings lately wrought, if only
you return having done it."

Beowulf, son of Ecgtheow, was open for business:
"No worries, wise one, I've got this. When a friend
needs to be avenged, it's better to fight than cry.
Even when mourning, this is how it goes.
We're all going to die, but most of us won't go out
in glory. Here's what matters, though, for men:
not living, but living *on* in legend. I'm not afraid.
1390 Stand up, protector of this place, and let us go together,
following Grendel's mother's tracks. I give you my fist:
she won't get away from Beowulf. There's no asylum,
no cleavage cracks in Mother Earth, no tree-barrow,
no ocean I can't find her in, wherever she hides.
Live through today, Hrothgar, it's the end of your miseries.
Be as brave as your scops say you are."

The old king stood and thanked God, mighty as ever,
for the promises of this prince. A horse was bridled
for Hrothgar, its mane knitted into war-braids,
1400 and the wise one, master of many, mounted
his sparkling steed, his status visible for miles.

His army followed on foot, shields raised,
pacing murderer's tracks, leaving their own uncovered;
they had no need to hide their hunting from her.
She'd gone overland, straight through the dark,
carrying the corpse of the comrade she'd killed, best beloved,
right-hand man, second set of eyes for Hrothgar.

The descendants of chieftains rode over razor-edged
rocks, through perilous passageways, places off-map,
1410 paths too slender for company, where sea monsters
sang and cliffs called for suicides. Hrothgar took
the front, his crew behind him, examining
her tracks, unhappily imagining the path ahead.
Finally, the trees leaned longingly toward
the stones, their needles bending as if to break,
a grove of ghosts. There was the mere,
water welling up like something wound-wrung,
red as blood. Though they'd known their man
was dead, they suffered afresh to discover
1420 in the mere a dark gift: there, at cliff's edge,
lay Æschere's head.

The company stared as water boiled with blood and bones.
A war-horn sounded, over and over, but the soldiers
sagged and sat down. The mere was full of monsters,
too many to mention: serpentine salt-dragons,

lizards in lethargy, lying on stones, the kinds of creatures
that surface seething in ships' wakes to bare teeth and twist
about an oar, foil fishers and bring bad omens to sailors.
The beasts dove, furious and frightened at the noise,
1430   the bugle and battlers' shouts, the shrillness of seekers
in their secret space. A Geat drew his bow and struck
a slithering one. An arrow piercing its scales, it struggled
and thrashed in the water. The other men, invigorated,
sought to join the killing; a second shot, a third,
then they slung themselves into the shallows
and speared it. *This* monster they could control.
They cornered it, clubbed it, tugged it onto the rocks,
stillbirthed it from its mere-mother, deemed it damned,
and made of it a miscarriage. They examined its entrails,
1440   awed and aggrieved.

Meanwhile, Beowulf gave zero shits.
He dressed himself in glittering gear,
his mail-shirt finely forged, links locked
and loaded. He'd meet this murdering mother
under mere, and amend her existence.
Even if she tried to smother him, his bone-cage
would stay intact. No weakness here. His helmet,
bright against the bleak backdrop, would save his skull
from the watery substrate, from the black mud
1450   and curious currents—hammered gold for a glamour-god,

made by one long gone, jewels and boar-shaped ornaments
imbued by the smith with power to keep other men from dying.
No battle-teeth could test it, no sword slice that shine.
Gold is good.

Last, but not least, Unferth, Hrothgar's left-hand man,
unexpectedly stanned for Beowulf, and handed him
his heirloom, Hrunting, an ancient hilted sword,
written with runes of ruin, iron blade
emblazoned with poison shoots, each bud
1460 reddened with enemy blood. In war, it never failed
to score flesh, had never been wrested from the fist
of him who held it. It was a sublime soldier's sword,
meant to limb enemies, and this wasn't the first time
it urged a hero to perform a feat.

Unferth sent his sword to the more skillful swordsman.
Note: the stone-bold son of Ecglaf had been blackout drunk
when he said that stuff he'd said, the rant he'd decanted
into Beowulf's ear. He wasn't man enough to dive
into rotten depths seeking someone so savage; he'd forgotten it
1470 now. He sought not to risk his skin, so surrendered
his chance at fame. Why sign up for endless night when
another man is armored, able, and ready to fight?

Couldn't be me

Beowulf, Ecgtheow's son, laid out his plan:

"My man, king of wisdom, ring-bringer, I'm about

to dive deep. Keep those words in mind,

the pledge we exchanged, that dearly done deal.

To recap: you, Halfdane's son, said that

I'm *your* son now, adopted and owned,

that if I died in this dive, you'd father me

1480   to a further shore. In short: I end up dead,

you pay my corps—feed them, pour them mead.

Also, adored Hrothgar, you swore

you'd send Hygelac my gold-get,

array for my Geat-lord the treasures I won,

and show him what keys this kingdom's

deeded me, what a generous giver you are,

what a son I was to you while I lived.

And Unferth! To that soldier I bequeath

my father-forged heirloom, my wave-winging

1490   war-blade. I'll gain fame with his Hrunting,

or be harvested by Hell."

The prince of Weather-Geats was done standing on ceremony.

He stepped to the mere's edge, and dove like a stone,

thrown not to skip, but to weight a ship-shrouded corpse.

Darkness drew him down. Most of a day was done

before he could see the contours of the bottom.

She who'd ruled these floodlands proudly for
a hundred seasons, ferocious, tenacious, rapacious,
yes, *she* felt his presence in her realm, and knew
1500 a man from above was invading the below.
She swam and seized him, but his body was swathed—
boar-helm, war-shirt—and she couldn't peel the mail off
to reveal his dread fate, nor impale him on fingernails.
She dragged him through dregs instead; the sea-wolf
slung the soldier out of the abyss and into her hall.
He was too tightly held to wield his sword, no matter how
he wished to war against her. As she swam, a shoal
came seeking to school him: a scrimshaw selection
of sea monsters, rising out of the dark, tunneling with
1510 tooth and tusk, spearing and jeering. Sharks, seals,
squealing beasts boring through the bog, biting
at his battle-shirt. The warrior squinted
in the shadows and made out the domed walls
of the hall, damming back the damned waters,
the mere made sere by engineering.
He saw the glow of a fire, brilliant light
flaming up and flaring, and then, at last,
he saw her: the reclusive night-queen,
the mighty mere-wife. Fearless, he heaved
1520 his sword to take her life, swinging with all
his strength so the edge rang against her skull,

but it was to no avail: his war-torch was dimmed,
his blood-boldness gone. She was impervious
to his blade. The sword had failed him,
though it'd served many worthy soldiers,
skinned many adversaries, slicing armor,
hacking helmets into hash. This was the first time
the heirloom hadn't overwhelmed an enemy.

Hygelac's heir was bent on blood, thinking
1530 of legacy, of legend. He hurled the sword:
useless hoard-gilt. Let it shatter in the silt.
He'd fight like a man, and take her hand to hand,
his fingertips blueprinting her skin. This is what
real men must do, come on, we all know the truth:
if you want to win, you have to forget you're afraid to die.

The Geat was ready to rumble, pissed now.
He roared a challenge, warmed for war with
Grendel's mother, twisting her hair around his fist,
raging, swinging her by her own skein, flinging
1540 her to crash against the kingdom she'd reigned over.
She rose again, relentless, and turned on him, gripping
and flipping him. The pugilist panicked. His certainty
crumbling, he took flight and fell. He began,
sick-hearted, to hear his death knell, his sure feet
fumbling, his fight-spirit fugitive.

She bent over his breast, held the hall-invader
hard to the stones, and drew a long knife. The mere-wife
meant to avenge her son, her sole heir, but Beowulf's mail
shielded him, his shoulder safe in the sclerite of some
1550 smith's genius, links staying locked to bend her blade.
Ecgtheow's heir would've been filleted, recategorized
as MIA, and left to rot in her cavern, had not his suit
saved him. That, too, was God's work.
The Lord, maker of miracles, sky-designer,
had no trouble leveling the playing field
when Beowulf beat the count and stood.

He glimpsed it hanging in her hoard, that armory
of heirlooms, somebody's birthright. A sword,
blessed by blood and flood, ancient, dating from
1560 the dawn of things, so tremendous only a hero
could heft it, though all would envy it. Beowulf gripped
the giant's sword at the hilt, and then he, the Scylding's
main man, in desperation, not expecting to exist after this
night, swung it at his enemy with all his might.

It was enough: he cleaved her spine. Those bone-rings
given by God were bitten through, the house of her head
raided, as her hall had been. She bent as though
    praying,

and was spent, sinking to the stones. The sword sweated red;
the swordsman regretted nothing.

1570 The light was strong now, a brilliance
like flame and tallow meeting in a sky
sick of sleep, and Beowulf took the volume
of the vault, itemizing everything,
his sword held high as defense
against any other awfulness that sought
him here. Hygelac's hit man had more
in mind. He sought to repay Grendel
for his wrath, for every night he'd spent
ravening, not just the first evening he'd come
1580 to Heorot, helping himself to fifteen
Danes and holding another fifteen hostage,
dragging them from home into horrors.
Against the far wall, our hero found Grendel,
still as a sleeper, war-riven,
a cadaver, cold and collapsed,
heartless after his time in Heorot.
Beowulf desecrated the dead,
swinging the sword again and again,
and rending the flesh, a heft, a wrench,
1590 removing Grendel's head.

Above, Hrothgar's men surrounded the mere,
holding the fort as best they could. Suddenly,
they saw the waters boil with blood, a roiling of gore,
salt, and sorrow. They lowered silvered heads.
"Oh no," said the old men, tightly packed
around their prince. That was a sad day.
They wept for lost wishes, sure they'd never see
Beowulf again, let alone witness him, in triumph,
presenting his kill to their king. The sea-wolf had
1600 savaged him, everyone agreed, and it was lunchtime.
The brave Scyldings forsook the cliff top and took
their gold-giver home, but the visiting Geats, now vagrant,
stayed—hopeless, heartsick, staring into the churning mere,
yearning against all evidence for their lord to reappear.

Below, in Beowulf's hands, the slaying-sword
began to melt like ice, just as the world thaws
in May when the Father unlocks the shackles
that've chained frost to the climate, and releases
hostage heat, uses sway over seasons to uncage
1610 His prisoner, Spring, and let her stumble into the sun.

The Geat's glory got nothing else from that estate,
though he eyeballed the treasures Grendel's mother
had collected. He took only head and hilt, jewel-scabbed
salvaged gilt. The blade itself had bled out,

the inscriptions on it smeared to smut, so scathing
was the blood of the slain stranger. It was done.
The man who'd made it through alive, survivor
of his enemy's annihilation, swam as fast
as he could swim, undoing his dark dive.
1620 The mere ran clear and pure, now
the ruler of the deep had unclasped her hand
from ephemeral existence, letting loose her life.

He surfaced at last, the hardy-hearted captain,
swimming to shore, reveling in the heft of his hoard,
the sea-chest he carried. Stunned, his men ran
to meet him, thanking all that was holy, his loyal
entourage rejoicing, shouting that he was risen,
their lord, their leader, their all. They undressed him,
freeing him of his armor, letting him breathe air
1630 instead of water. The mere was peaceful now,
though battle-pinked, reflecting the cloudy sky above.

Hearts singing with love, they returned
from stranger's country by twisted trails,
lapping the Earth with strides onto known roads,
safe roads. The boldest men among them
carried Grendel's head, a hard task,
heaving it onto the heath from over sea-cliffs.
These men were major, massive, and committed.

71

is that so much to ask for?

Four brave warriors paired off to bear the gore hallward,
1640   a skull spitted on a spear-litter. They approached
Heorot together, celebrating as they went,
fourteen ferocious, war-worked Geats, trampling
down the meadow, Beowulf among them,
blending into his brothers, matching step for step.

That leader of men entered the hall a hero,
and made his way to Hrothgar, grit-written.
His crew dragged Grendel's head into the mead-hall,
where a meal was being served, and a host of lesser men
ferried cups to mouths. In their midst was the queen of the house,
1650   their hoard, their treasure. The Danes stared, jaws dropped.

Beowulf made a speech to end all speeches, that son of Ecgtheow.
"So, we're back from the brink, Halfdane's son, Scyldings'
    savior,
bringing you this token of our esteem, sea-booty, gore-loot,
no big whoop. Here's to glory! And now, my story. *gross*
I don't mean to say this shit was no thing. I lived through
your basic fistfight underwater, a tryst with destruction.
I did the deed you deemed necessary, but I'd be bluffing
if I didn't say I would've died had God not kept me close.
Though my sword seemed severe, I'd have been helpless,
1660   had I had only Hrunting. Hard-core as it is, it failed
when I brought it to battle. God gave me grace—He sometimes

72

saves the solitary—on a ledge glowed another blade,
marvelous enough to mend the mistake I'd made
trying to take on Grendel's mother in her own lair-lake.
Speed was my only advantage, solo as I was. I snatched
the sword, striking down the bitch that sought
to slay me, scoring the other, too, her son. The blade
blistered as it touched their blood, and rivers of red
rushed over it, unforging it from fire-fang, into what
1670 you see here, a bladeless hilt. I brought it from below,
having avenged the Danes' death. That's all I need to say,
except that I promise you and every nobleman here, your sleep
is safe now. Your corps can defend you, whether brave boys
or bold men—you need not worry for their lives or longevity,
Lord of Scyldings, nor fear anyone surging up from the mere.
We're done with that damage."

The hilt was handed off into the hard hands
of the ring-lord, a relic older than any ruler,
rendered in iron by giants, and inherited, after
1680 enemies perished, by the Danish king.
When the gruesome Grendel gave up the ghost,
when God won over him and his mother, when that
murderous pair was rendered moribund, it made sense
that such a sweet piece, this smith-struck sword,
would go to the prince, the loftiest lord between
the salt seas, the guy who gave the greatest gifts on Earth.

Hrothgar considered his convictions. He handled the hilt,
an ancient thing, a fossil from forgotten days,
squinting at the legend left there for the literate.
1690 It was engraved with an epic inscrutable to him,
the story of how war woke in the world, and a flood brewed,
drowning the race of giants, placing them beneath the waves,
a punishment for others, poor Lord-lacking unbelievers,
sin-soaked strangers, severed from sanctuary.
On the golden guard, the runes were written perfectly,
the true name of the sword's first owner,
long since ash, for whom it had been forged,
with its twisted hilt and serpent-slipped steel.
There was silence until Halfdane's son spoke.

1700 "A ruler who's been known as a good man since
days of old, a generous, just gift-giver, a war-wielding
homeland healer, is equipped to say the following:
this man's as good a man as me. Beowulf, my boy!
You've proven yourself in every context. Your name
will be known around the world. You're steady, strong,
and sure in all respects. I open my arms to you, as agreed,
and fulfill the bonds of friendship. For your people,
you'll be, like me, a defender and a hero.
But . . . hold up, hear me out, indulge me a moment.
1710 Heremod, that old king, was no hopeful hero to the heirs

of Ecgwela, the Honor-Scyldings. His rise was their fall.
He raged, cut down close comrades, aged advisers,
and when he died, he died galled and alone, friendless,
though famous. God had given him grace—granted him
wealth, health, and power. His road had no rocks on it.
He'd known only joy. Somehow, though, his heart
was not a hawk but a drone. He bombed his own bases,
denied his Danes damages, kept entrenched in combat.
He commanded his kingdom's collapse, and was, when ancient,
1720 loathed where he could've been loved, his life lesioned
with losses. Listen to me, boy. Keep your shit straight.
I've been fostered by frost-seasons, fathered by time,
and I'm dropping knowledge now.

"Here's one of the world's wonders: God is good.
He's given us gifts—the capacity for clarity granted our kind.
He runs the show, though, manages every aspect of existence.
Sometimes He gives a man from a good clan room to roam
wherever he desires, every instant filled with joy,
lets him run his own kingdom and rule over boys
1730 who guard his borders, stand-up guys who'd die for him.
God does this for so many decades that the man himself,
because men in the end are fools, forgets how things work.
He shirks his soul-keeping. There'll be no changes for *him*,
he thinks, no end in sight, no loss of love or life.
He wallows like a bear in honey, unstung,

and nothing scathes him, not sickness nor sorrow,

nor does his mood darken, nor do his enemies find him,

their blades sharp and stealthy, no—instead the world

wends to his will. He notices nothing nasty in himself,

1740　until one day everything changes.

Every guard goes down eventually,

sagging on the stone wall surrounding the soul.

Here, while the sentry's sleeping, a sniper strikes,

sending a spike into the man's heart. Now he's poisoned,

selfishness searing his certainty—he's never needed

to defend himself against internal threats, but the greedy orders

of this beastly boss make him think the halls he's guarded,

the treasures he's watched over for decades, are nothing

compared to what he deserves. He hoards, hisses,

1750　hides his gold, refuses support to those who've served

him. He forgets his debts, Fortune's amnesiac,

blacking out bounty in favor of bitterness.

Turn to the end of the story: I'll wait.

His body weakens, fails, falls. An inheritor

crawls into his throne and passes that king's heirlooms,

his protected and precious things, to anyone he wishes to woo,

no regard for the dead man's worth, rituals, or requirements.

"Armor yourself against that kind of idiocy, my brave boy,

my Beowulf. Keep yourself on an even keel, aiming

1760　your ambition at eternity, instead of the everyday.

Don't let avarice override intelligence. It's only a season
that a young soldier's strength stays stalwart—
before plague or blade bring obsolescence. A crackling
blaze, a rush of waves, a slippery sword-grip,
a spear soaring silently through the air,
or even the ague of age. Your gaze will darken, too, boy.
Your world will dim. Death will kneel over you eventually,
and solicit your surrender.

"Hear me now. I ruled the Ring-Danes
1770 for fifty years, fighting adversaries, holding borders,
our spears and swords against assassins of every nation,
until I thought my enemies were casualties, Earth
emptied of them. I relaxed into comfort and fortune,
and just as we celebrated our conquering every kingdom,
then, *then* came Grendel. He waited in the darkness,
invaded my inner sanctum with savagery, broke my spirit,
and drove me into a dark depression.
Thank God, thank all that is holy, I lived long enough
to see you bring me Grendel's head, sword-split
1780 after years of struggle. Now I can look upon it,
crow, and count him a corpse . . .
Oh, but I've gone on too long.
Sit down, golden boy, heir of this hall. Feast. There'll be
more rewards in the morning, from my hands to yours."

Beowulf grinned, and took his assigned seat,
set by his elder king. A bench bedecked in Beowulf!
Then the Danes and Geats got down to business.
The celebration began in earnest—the room was filled
and a banquet bowed the tables. Night hooded the hall
1790 and wrapped all who celebrated in starry dark.
At last, the companions rose—their elder was ebbing—
and called for sleep. The Geat followed suit,
weary after warfare, heartsick for home,
accompanied by a hall-officer who led him
from the company, there to tend to every desire,
a butler of burdens, bleaching away bloodshed
and battle, packing off pain.
It was no more than Beowulf deserved.
He dove into dreams, as above him
1800 the hall stretched toward Heaven, its gilt
and vaulted ceilings shielding the hero's heart.

At dawn, a black raven called out the melody of morning,
the happiness of inhabiting the heavens. Sunlight snatched
    shadows
from corners, and wayward warriors readied themselves
for removal—hungering for home. Their leader was up at
    once,
looking into the distance, his soul seeking his ship.

The fierce fighter called for Hrunting to be brought,
and bade Unferth receive it, with thanks for the loan.
He complimented its blade, and said it had been
1810 a friend to him, powerful in battle. He mentioned
nothing about the dullness of the edge—
he had no urge to nurture a grudge.

Now the warriors were ready to roll, armor on,
hearts set on home. Their prince approached the dais
where the king awaited, and knelt at Hrothgar's feet,
confident and canny.

Beowulf (Ecgtheow's own) said the proper words:
"It's time for us who set sail to save this king's land,
to tell you we're overdue to return to our own man,
1820 Hygelac. At Heorot, we've been held as kin,
hosted, kept comfortable, and if there's anything more
I can do for you, beyond the battles I've won,
any more of your heart I can win by warring,
demand it: your wish is my command.
If I ever hear a whisper over the whale-road
that your walls are wobbling, that neighbors
are invading, that enemies are afoot, as enemies
are wont to be, I'll appear with a horde of thousands,
and bring them to bear. Hygelac may not be gray
1830 like you, he may seem young to rule, but know this—

he has my back. He'll heed my call if you need help,
and bring speech and sword to support me, assisting you
with any needs, as you would me—your new son.
I'll bring a spear-forest, a ferocious force,
should you need fighters. And if your son Hrethric
should come to foster in Geatland, a Dane-king's voyager
in Hygelac's court, he'll find friends there.
Foreign shores share their secrets
with those who are themselves worthy."

1840 Overcome, Hrothgar answered him:
"The Lord, all-knowing, put words in your mouth,
Beowulf, words of love. I've never heard a boy—a man—
manage such diplomacy, such propriety, so easily.
Your body's made of steel, your mind mercury,
your tongue gold, and if Hrethel's son should—
I'm not saying he will—die in battle, a sword,
spear, or sickness slaying that princely protector
of your kind, and you remain alive, I'm certain
with all I know that the Geats would never find
1850 a better man to be their well-won king and protector,
if you should want that level of lordship,
that intense responsibility.
I like you more every moment, Beowulf.
You've bonded two tribes.
The Danes and Geats are peace-woven now,

80

despite our harrowing history.

We've fought fiercely in the past,

but now we're friends forever.

As long as I'm king of this remote place,

1860 my treasury will spill into your coffers—

all that's mine on offer, from sea to shining sea.

All the ships that cross will carry gifts to you.

I know now what I did not before—your people

are like my people, perfect and prized,

defenders of the good against the god-awful."

The Dane's defender dropped gold in the hand

of the Geat's glory, twelve treasures more

given in health and wealth, and bid him

take himself to shore now, but come back

1870 anytime. The old king had run out of ceremonies.

He kissed his new best boy, his adopted kin,

throwing his arms about his neck and weeping.

Two premonitions overtook him, shaking him

to the core, the stronger one that they'd never meet again.

Beowulf was so dear to him he couldn't

stop trembling—but in his heart and mind's eye,

he foresaw that keeping this savior son nearby

could only end in flame. He opened his arms.

He let him go.

1880 Beowulf went forth, a golden warrior
striding across green grasses. While peering
off cliffs, he tallied his rewards. His ship
waited impatiently on him, tugging at her anchor.
All the gifts given by Hrothgar would be weighed
as they went on. "That was a good king," his men agreed,
perfect in every way, until time, robber of vaults,
stole his strength and swapped it for softness.

Down they marched to the shore, bright boys reveling
in metal dress and battle-gains, stamping in glee.
1890 The land-watch took note of them from afar,
as he had at their arrival, this time without rancor—
he raised his hand and rode in greeting, arriving
as they boarded their vessel, gifts glinting in sunlight.
He announced to the assembled that the departing heroes
would surely be celebrated in Geatland. They pulled
the ship to sand and filled it with a king's ransom:
gems and gold, horses and armor, the mast marking
the spot of their treasure. They hefted Hrothgar's heirlooms
whole cloth into the hold, gifting even the coastguard
1900 a sword, gold-wrapped and gorgeous, so that later
he'd be able to flash it while drinking,
and say he'd been there when.

They shoved the ship from the spit, keel splashing
into salt, Denmark soon distant. Sails whipped
about her mast, a veil for her sea-gaze.
Ropes tautened and timbers moaned.
Winds surged to skip the vessel like a
smooth stone across the ocean, white with foam,
lifted by light, until at last the cry was heard,
1910   the cliffs of Geatland grown visible, counted,
claimed, and the ship sang out for the final
push, thrusting herself at the shore,
shoving keel at country.

Their harbor-watcher was already running,
waiting as he'd been for days, eyes peeled
for the return of his tribe. He tugged
anchor cables, moored the ship to sand,
heaving her against the current to keep
the waves from seducing her again. He ordered
1920   that the holds be emptied, gold and gems,
all stores and hoards straight to shore.

After that it was only a hop-skip to Hygelac,
Hrethel's heir, and the gold would go his way,
up the cliff to king and company.
The building was brilliant, the king imposing,

enthroned in his home-hall. Hygd, his queen,

was young but shrewd. Though she'd only

overwintered recently in the realm, Hæreth's daughter

knew her duty: open heart met open hands when it came

1930   to Geats. She paid attention, made trenchant thrift

feel more generous than lessers' over-gifts.

Nothing like Modthryth, <u>oh shit, remember her?</u>   *NO???*

The people's princess, an utter criminal.

Bro, if anyone even *looked* at her in daylight,

save her own overlord, <u>she'd deal that man death</u>—

order him bound, each shackle tightened to torture,

his sentence resounding from on high: sword-selection,

then the entertainment, a public flaying, arteries spurting,

gore, good riddance. She may have been beautiful,

1940   she may have been royal, but can we agree here?

Why the brutality?! Pretty peace-weavers aren't meant

to claw, bringing good men down just for looking,

innocent oglers sent deathward. Talk about inflated offenses!

Right. Then Hemming's son became Modthryth's husband,

and she shifted mysteriously. Drinkers spilt a different song—

a bathroom-wall graffiti-shrift. Marriage mellowed

the monster. <u>She sea-changed when she was Offa's wife</u>.

Everyone liked her better. Her father had traded her,

hauled her onto a ship, dowry-gowned, conveyed her

1950   from her homeland to other shores. Her nature

changed when she got free of her family.

She became queenly; before she'd been the worst.
She sat on her new throne, famed for kindness,
loyalty, devotion to her king. And him? Bro, obviously
he was the best, a king among kings, and moreover,
the greatest man who ever lived, if that's not overkill,
so it's no wonder she learned morals under his hand,
Offa's honored wife, as he ruled over his lands.
From that duo, as proof, if needed, came a good son,
1960 Eomer, grandson of Garmund, Hemming's kinsman,
well-met to all warriors, reliable in combat,
and a keeper of comrades.

Back to Beowulf, a hero himself, marching with his men
across the sand, crossing the sprawling strand,
the tidal flats and salted shores, making haste
beneath brightness as the sky-candle shone hard
from the south. They hurried blur-fast overland
to where, rumor had it, their youthful king,
killer of Ongentheow, protector of his own clans,
1970 was handing out booty in his honored hall.
That Beowulf was back, was shouted man to man,
so Hygelac knew it, even as his warrior made his way
through the gates and into the hall, war-kin to the king
and killer captain, well and willing.

The hall was cleared and the king awaiting,
as our boy and his horde marched in.
Hygelac greeted his warrior in formal speech,
then sat down head-to-head with him,
ready to compare notes with his returning
1980 boatman-brother. Hæreth's daughter wafted wifely
through the hall, mead-jug held in her hands,
caring for the companions, pouring a waterfall
into cups as warriors held them high. Only then
did Hygelac begin to question his comrade, calmly,
commandingly, to glean the story of the war-Geats,
and take the tale for his own hall-history.

"Holy hell, Beowulf, how'd it go out there?
You left with hardly a word, and hied yourself
overwater to defend a hall not your home: Heorot.
1990 And Hrothgar? Did you help him? We know his woes,
and to be honest, I thought them insoluble.
I've been mourning you in advance, dreading news
of your death. As you may recall, I begged you
to let the Danes do their own damn dirty work.
It's them who began a blood feud with Grendel,
and them who should end it. Well, thank God
you're home, whatever horror
happened at Heorot."

Beowulf, descendant of Ecgtheow, began:

2000 "I'm surprised you haven't heard what went down,

Hygelac. It was proud; already written

into poems. Grendel and I slammed each other

in the very hall he'd been harrowing, murdering

medal-Scyldings, ripping hearts from their holds,

all of which, not to jump ahead, he got whipped

into eternity for. Grendel will never have a single son

to brag on his daddy's battles, to tell the tale

of our night-fight, no matter whether any of his

awful line manage to live through a shifting

2010 civilization. Lemme lay it out now.

When I got to Denmark, I sped to Hrothgar's hall

and presented myself, giving cred and clan.

Once he knew who I was, and what I'd come to do,

he stationed me on a bench between his own sons

and threw a raucous feast for me. I've never seen

any company drunker or more delighted.

'More mead, men!' The queen herself came through,

that pretty peace-pleader, and gave out gifts

to bolster courage—a war-torc for this warrior—

2020 before she snuggled up beside the king.

Hrothgar's daughter, too, made the rounds,

bringing beer to the highest rank, all plank-arranged.

'Freawaru!' they called, and she circled the room,

offering up a studded cup. That bangle-bedecked beauty

is betrothed to Froda's bereaved son, Ingeld.
The Scyldings' king chose him for her husband,
Hrothgar hoping, kingdom-keeper that he is,
that sending his precious daughter to fuck his foe's son
will fix the fatherly feud: heal bitter hearts and bandage
2030 weeping wounds. But spears seldom sleep for long
when a ruler's fallen, no matter how perfect the princess.

"We can predict how the Heotho-Bards will react,
every loyal thane there. All will go well, until after
the wedding, when the young lord stands to dance,
and dips his Danish bride, her body dripping
in a dark dowry, ancient garnets bought in blood
from the Heotho-Bards themselves, sparkling stones
stripped from beloved ghosts, ring-mail wrought
by their own ancestors, cherished heirlooms
2040 returning home as Danish dazzle, uncredited.
An aged uncle, already drunk, swaying, will shout:
'Let's have a toast!'
His eyes will focus on rings well known to him,
triggering black thoughts of massacre, all that killing,
all those spirits, suddenly filling the hall. Heart pounding,
he'll sound the sorrows of his people, begin to prick
the prince's conscience, seeking to stir him.
'To our host! And to the sword his father carried
in his final battle! Don't tell me you don't recognize

2050 the prime iron he died swinging, that day he fought

the Danes. Let me refresh your memory, boy.

The day Withergyld was murdered, and our heroes fell

to folly, the day the Scyldings shook the field down,

scavenging our dead. Now who wears your father's armor?

Some assassin's son, walking into our home-hall,

shaking sword and status, boasting that he owns us,

weighted with the wonders you should yourself be wearing.'

"He won't stop, but will keep pressing,

raising the temperature of the room,

2060 until one of the Danish lady's thanes is slain,

streaked with crimson, killed for Danish deeds,

his slayer sprinting out alive, into home territory.

This will begin it all again. Both sides, vow-bound,

will break, old thirsts unslaked, a rage rising in Ingeld,

his love for Freawaru frozen, comforts gone to curses.

That's all just to say, sidebar, that the Heotho-Bards

aren't to be trusted, their faltering friendship with the Danes

bridged only by a bride.

"Now, my main man, let me get back to Grendel,

2070 the story of our clash and crash, everything

that happened when we two went hand to hand.

After Heaven's gem slipped smoothly down to soil,

he arrived: that froth-fanged foulness,

that twilight-tormentor, come to attack us
as we gathered in silent safety in Heorot.

was it safe??

There, Handsceoh was fated to fall,
torn from his life, first-cursed on this quest.
Our beloved brother was beaten and eaten,
his gory grave Grendel's gullet. Lemme be clear:
2080 Grendel ate him up. The attacker's teeth
were bloody, his face strewn with gobbets,
his body swollen with evil, and still
he wasn't finished feasting, but insisted
on leaving the golden hall with more harvest.
Grendel was famous for his heft: he extended hands,
then, for none other than your boy. He had a huge sack
hanging from his shoulder, stitched with sinew,
clasped with clever workings, crafted of twisted
dragon skins. Grendel knew nothing of us,
2090 but this wrath-wanderer wanted to stuff
Beowulf and his boys into that sack, abduct us.
That shit wasn't happening. The moment I stood
to face him, my rage evident, Grendel was a goner.
I'd be talking too long if I got into every detail
of the battle, how I paid him in pain for wrongs
done to Danes. Suffice it to say, I won you honor,
my king, and the Geats as well. Even though Grendel
got loose and lived, suckling at survival's sweetness

a little longer, his right arm stayed in Heorot
2100 holding the door, amputated, and he limped,
anguished, to the mere, where he dove
and drowned in despair.

"The Dane-lord rewarded me for my life-risking
with piles of gold and heaps of heirlooms,
once the sun was up. All of us at table,
primed for entertainment—singers and story-slingers.
An ancient Scylding, steeped in the history of
his people, told tales of the early days.
Sometimes one of the men touched harpstrings,
2110 recounting his life story, and other times the king himself
offered up an awesome riff, while in turn the grimmest
among us, scarred and wizened, would hobble up to tell
of boyhood battles, then shift to songs of old age,
overcome by emotion, silvered heart aching
for the good old golden days.   *its giving Madeleine*

"We reveled indoors for hours, joyful and united,
until nightfall came stalking us, a shadowy reaper.
Uninvited, she appeared, a dame made of damage.
Grendel's mother slinking out of dark, formatted for fury,
2120 avenging her son and bringing ruin back to the room.
Grief and death-theft had possessed her, and she came

91

to find the Geats who'd found her Grendel. She marched
for blood, a rebel warrior entering private premises, and
    captured
a counselor, Æschere, the king's closest and wisest.
In the morning, there was no body to burn, no corpse,
nothing at all to call back his memory in smoke,
nor limbs to light for love. She'd borne his flesh away
and hidden it in the darkness under the mountain
and rushing waters, her mere-morgue.
2130 Hrothgar was broken by this blow, worse than any other,
his scars reopened by razors. The king begged me—
yes, begged, and he named you, too—to go after her,
to pursue her underwater to avenge his loss,
and if I did it, to gain even greater glory. He named his price,
and it was done. Into icy waters I went, diving deep to meet
my match, and found her, raging. I took her and she took me, too,
hand to hand, woman to man, water roaring red,
splitting the current with color, until at last, in her own hall,
I beheaded Grendel's mother with a sword too substantial
2140 for anyone else's swing. I barely left with my life, and only that
by Fate's choice, but when I returned to the surface,
Halfdane's heir, bearer of men, gave me a stocked store
of his own hoard, gifts golden and godly.

"Thus Hrothgar acted as ever he has, paying me
for my sacrifice and more, letting me set my wages

in goblets and goods. From Hrothgar's heirlooms
comes Hygelac's inheritance. I've brought these gifts
to you, your majesty, and I give them willingly.
You're the man I seek to impress.
2150 I've got no other family left, none close.
Your kindness is my comfort."

Beowulf called for the boar's head standard, the battle-crested
helmet, the grizzled gray mail-shirt, and the ferocious
    war-sword,
and wrought an account of their provenance.

"When Hrothgar gave me all these precious things,
brilliant leader, he bade me bring you words as well,
to explain why they're favors fit for kings.
He told me this had belonged to his older brother,
King Heorogar, but he'd kept it locked away,
2160 never giving it over to inheritance, not even to
his son Heoroweard, despite his worthiness,
despite his loyalty. Now it's yours to bear in health!"

Bro, here's what I know: four horses were brought in next,
presented to the king. Beowulf bestowed those bays,
along with their armor, each one an impossible gift
of blood and girth. This is how it should be between
birth-kin, no plots, no plans for plunder,

no conspirers crafting catastrophe, no one
sculpting death where life should be.
2170 The warrior-king, Beowulf's uncle, was lucky
to have the loyalty of his nephew, and he carried
Beowulf's burdens in return.

I heard Beowulf brought Hygd the golden torc
gifted him by Wealhtheow, and with it, three horses
harnessed similarly in gold, sleek and graceful. The queen
wore her reins well, her breast radiant with heroic history.

Thus did Beowulf bring his bravery to bear—
he'd battled like a brawler, but could hold court
with kings and queens, too, never punching down,
2180 never mocking drunk comrades, never locking himself
in combat with those whose strength couldn't stand.
He kept his stones controlled, and when he rolled,
he rolled only with equals. Mind, he hadn't had this status
when he left, a boy who men looked on as low—
the Geats thought him lazy, and even their lord
had never given him span on the beer-bench, believing
he was all bluster, no badass, thinking his position came
from privilege, not class. But now? Everyone who'd thought
Beowulf was just a wayward boy got taught.

2190   The king, war-bringer, protector of men, ordered
        Hrethel's heirloom brought in, and that splendid
        sword, gem-clotted, the best by far in the treasury,
        he lay in Beowulf's lap. Then more! He gave
        his man seven thousand hides of land,
        and a hall of his own, into which he could
        place his throne. They both already had land
        from their fathers, ancestral sway, but now,
        a better way: land came from Hygelac
        to his new right hand, Beowulf.

2200   Later days were cloudier. A war began.
        Hygelac was dead by then, his shield yielding
        no safety for his son, Heardred, against the war-wired
        Scylfings, who patrolled, hunting for the young Geat-king.
        They found him surrounded by his soldiers, slew them,
        and after that, boys—well, you know.

        The rings rolled down to Beowulf. He caught the kingdom
        he'd rejected, and held tight to it for fifty winters,
        before he, too, found himself an old man,
        the gray guardian of Geatland.

2210   Across a star-studded sky, in deepest dark one night,
        a dragon ranged, unchecked. She was a scar-skinned

warrior, long accustomed to shadow-soaring by moonlight,

defending her claim, hoarding in her own high hall.

No man knew the way into the dragon's cliff-top cocoon,

but a thief stumbled through a split in the stone,

and retrieved a gem-glistering goblet. He robbed

her of nothing else, just the cup—but.

Up she rose, raging, grieving, though to cry out

was to confess she'd been stripped while sleeping.

2220 This country, these creatures, would feel her fire.

The instigator hadn't intended to ignite Armageddon;

he'd merely slunk into a cave, and found a crypt. This slave,

seeking safety from a miserly master, became the spark

that smoked a primeval monarch out. He spelunked into
     yawning dark,

and gripped a wall. Instead of clammy stone, he felt a kiln;

instead of granite, gold. Whose forbidden hold was this?

What had he provoked? He wrapped trembling fingers around

the first small, shining thing he found, and fled. For the vault

was more than a treasury: piles of preciouses nested

2230 beneath the coils of a snoring serpent. It was a bed.

Bro, no one living knows the name of the lost soul

who'd interred those spoils long ago, burying the grave

goods of a wealthy race. Death had snatched them all

into a sack and lifted them out of existence, leaving

only one, this ghost-custodian, mourning
over friends, family, foes alike. He had no future
for himself in mind, nothing but a dead end.
Left with only this haul of tomb-treasure,
nothing to spend it on, no joys left to consume,
2240 he attempted to wring pleasure from his stint
as the richest man alive. There was a barrow
already built, high on a headland above the sand,
secured by waves against trespass. The last man
climbed the slope, carrying his collection, all the things
worth saving, all the wonders he could find. He
organized the bounty, performing final rites.

"Hold these, Mother Earth. Men have lost
their grip. We mined this metal from you,
forged it for fighting, ruined ourselves warring
2250 against one another. Man by man, we gave our souls
over to spite, lives flashing before our eyes, farewells
to all our hopes. I'm alone here now, no sword-bearer,
no cup-keeper, no hall-sweeper. My flock's
flown south without me. This hard helmet will lose
its filigree—there's no polisher waiting
to keep our battle-masks gleaming. Everyone
once waking now dreams. This breastplate
endured many battles—bruised by blades, smashed
by shields—now it'll be red dust, along with its owner.

2260 Metal shells rest here without their warriors.
Now there are no heroes, no soothing music,
no harp, no hawk soaring through hall,
no swift horses trampling green grass.
We existed; now we're extinct."

And so the last survivor mourned, making his way
from emptiness to emptiness, listing his sins one by one,
wandering the world woefully, until death came
welling in, to wash him from the rocks.

Afterward, an ancient collector soaring through
2270 the starry hours happened past, and saw a golden
glyph from above. A flame-tongued one who sought
out strongholds as she scourged, a slip-skinned dragon,
tagging the sky with flaming sigils. Farmers kept vigil,
dreading her smoky signs. She was hungry for hoards,
tempted by temples, and every burial site
was known by her to hold heathen hopes,
howling for a new owner.

There she dwelt, this nameless fear, for three hundred years,
padlocking her hall with all her limbs until the infiltrator
2280 infuriated her. That slave skittered to the owner's home
with the stolen goblet, and gifted it to get mercy.
Thus, the hold of the old gold-get was known,

her vault cataloged, her ring-hoard wrung.
For the master clocked what he was looking at,
a treasure protected by time.

At once, the dragon woke, choking on fury.
She huffed her hoard, winding herself around it,
revulsion kindling within her, the sour scent
of an enemy man, the footprints of a plunderer,
2290 who'd blundered past her sleeping skull and seen
her secret dreaming-place. We all know stories
like this one: a man unmarked by Fate may sometimes
cloak himself in God's grace, passing close to monsters,
unbeheld. The hoard-holder fine-toothed the ground,
fire-foraging for the man who'd invaded her bedchamber.
Wide she circled, planning his disemboweling,
claw-mapping every inch of wilderness,
though no man there to capture. She imagined
a wild battle, flexed rapturously, then undulated
2300 into her lair to hunt again for the missing cup
only to rediscover the telltale evidence:
someone had desecrated her delights.
Teeth gritted, she ticked until nightfall,
that guardian of old gold and haunted history,
her urge toward murder more intense by the moment.
Eventually, ecstatic, she outlasted the light.
Into darkness she emerged and put the world on blast,

roaring into the sky, a comet of catastrophe.

Villagers in the vicinity felt her attack first,

2310 their lands blackened, but soon it would be their

lord and treasure-giver suffering.

The dragon swooped low and spat flame, destroying

both manor and hovel, scrawling red RSVPs in the sky.

The winged wringer had no time for survivors. She skywrote

her grievances, then rewrote them roughly in land-fire

from end to end of Geat-realm, her scaly helm

shining as she sang insults from the clouds.

Back to her ridge she whipped as the sun showed itself,

slithering into her gold-stock, locking herself away.

2320 She'd exhaled upon their ground, and now they burned,

black blood, bah! She slept, trusting in human frailty

to keep her lair unmolested. That trust would turn

to dust, like everything.

Soon Beowulf received a blistering missive.

His own hall, his heart-home, had combusted.

He'd been ghost-throned by the skyborne gold-holder.

To the good man, this region's ring-giver, this was

distress unbearable—punishment, perhaps, from the Lord.

Unjust? He worried, weighed it: Had he broken

2330 old covenants? Unwarded his soul? Doubt dawned

as he considered deeds long done, sins kept secret.
He wasn't used to feeling insecure.

Meanwhile, the firedrake raked coast-to-coast
with claws, charred gilded Geatland without pause,
crimson blazes and black billows, until
the old war-king woke to action, plotting vengeance
on the stranger. The foremost warrior projected
for his own protection a myth-worthy shield,
made entirely of iron. He knew no forest-gift
2340 could defend him; his safety lay in smithy.
Linden couldn't withstand lightning. Though Beowulf
didn't predict he'd die in this fight, he and the dragon both,
he'd always known that Fate could fuck a fighter up,
no matter the hoards he'd held, no matter the luck he'd had.

The ring-collector was too proud to bring a war-band,
to march an army against the firmament-flier.
His plan would be his pyre—he imagined the dragon
a dimwit, clocking neither her courage nor her grit.
I mean, he had, for years, been up in it,
2350 persevering through pain and danger,
countless grim battles since he'd saved
Hrothgar and Heorot, since he'd rushed
Grendel and all his kin, knocking that

damned family to the mat. One of the worst
of those hand-to-hand hells had been the one
when Hygelac, Geat-king, closest comrade,
perished in Friesland. His skin became sheath
for a sword, his skull a cup overflowing
with blood. Beowulf saved himself
2360 only by swimming, fleeing the massacre
by sea, bearing back as he swam thirty suits
of armor torn from corpses he'd created.
The Hetware had no joy of him, hiding their heads
beneath their own splintering linden, as Beowulf
ground them into cold sand.
Few saw home again.

Solitary, salt-scourged, he swam screaming
over open ocean, Ecgtheow's son repatriating
grief-stricken to his homeland. Hygd tried
2370 to quicken him with the throne, offering him gold,
gemstones, a potent position, a life less lonely.
Her own son she didn't trust to govern,
to keep borders trussed against deploying hordes,
now his daddy was dead. She couldn't convince
Beowulf to step over Heardred, nor consent
to come to her bed, but instead he offered
his counsel to the boy-king, until he was
man enough to rule the Weder-Geats himself.

Soon thereafter, exiles appeared over the salt-highway,
2380 Ohthere's sons, who'd raised a coup against their
old wave-king, Onela. He was the ruler of the
Scylfings, had given gold from his kingdom seat,
was master of their mead-hall. Heedless, Heardred
received the refugees, and traded his life for it,
his reception repaid in regrets. A fatal flash of Onela's sword,
and Hygelac's line was ended. The Swede-king, satisfied,
set off to the briny boulevard, and Beowulf, bereaved,
ascended the Geat-throne, in grief, never surrendering
his reluctance to become the ruler.
2390 That was a good king.

In later days, our man paid the killers in kills,
avenging his dead prince by befriending Eadgils,
the last of the Swedish rebel sons. Beowulf sent him
an army of seaborne swords, and tied a scarlet ribbon
around the blood feud, exterminating Onela.

And so, Ecgtheow's heir inherited a complement of king's
qualifiers, dangers rare, treasures tragic, constant proofs
of courage, excelling at every impossibility,
until the day came for him to kill the dragon.

2400 The Geat-king rode with eleven companions,
     firing himself into fury as he hunted the lair's location.
     By then he'd found the smoking gun, the embezzlement
     that'd stoked the dragon's rage. The gilt cup had been
     brought to him by the burglar who'd begun this,
     and that thief, on life-tilt, became the thirteenth man,
     rife with regrets, compelled to guide an expedition
     back to the scene of his crime. The unwilling guest
     of the king led the rest, in safety of daylight,
     to the hide he'd strayed into, a golden grave
2410 near salt shoals and trembling tides. Piled
     inside, like scales, were mounds
     of etched metal, detailed by the dead,
     along with a veteran guardian,
     who now never slept. She was the
     sole barrier to entry, but burrowed beneath
     the earth as she was, there was no simple way
     to bring death to her den.

     The old king fell to his knees on the cliff point
     and willed good fortune upon the Geats he'd ruled,
2420 those who'd sat fireside, warmed by his gold.
     Stricken, suddenly unsteady, he foresaw his fate
     in the fog, shrouded but certain. For a moment,
     he felt for his old foes, fen-bound, embarking alone.

Soon, soon, his own lease would expire,
evicting him from hall, hearth, and home.

Beowulf, Ecgtheow's own son, manned up,
mastered himself, said it straight:
"I lived whole lives in my youth, endless combat,
great wars. I remember every moment, even now.
2430 When I was seven, my father sent me out to sleep
in the king's house. He dropped me on a new daddy,
King Hrethel, who kept me safe, opened his hands,
treated me, a fosterling, like his own sons.
Never was I less dear to him than Herebeald,
or Hæthcyn, or even my best-beloved Hygelac.
The eldest, Herebeald, tumbled into an early grave,
done in by his brother: Hæthcyn tugged his bone-bow,
flinging a missile that missed the mark,
shark-toothed his sibling's heart, a bloody thorn.
2440 There was no way to mourn for him, no vengeance
to be had, for what could mitigate the blame?
Who was left to shame for this
heart-thieving? Nobody.

"It's the same sort of sorrow when a man outlives
his son, sees him climb the gallows and swing,
sentenced, justly, for crimes against the king.

The father hollers out a sob to rapturing ravens,
witnesses his boy swallowing dust, unable to plead
his case. No settlement in silver can buy a child back
2450 from the gods of air. The father awakens disgraced,
in despair thereafter, knowing his inheritor's been
erased. He has no verve, no urge to visit beds,
no wish to father a new son, now his firstborn's dead.
He stares in sorrow at his child's empty room, hears
the dreary wind that habits there now. His hall is silent,
cheerless, hungry, hearth without coals, riders sagging
in their saddles, heroes hidden, where once singers sang
and harps were fingered, where a yardful of sons were brothers.
Abandoned on Earth, left to live alone, with only sins
2460 to number, the gray king retreats to slumber, moaning dirges.
What son? What wife? What life? What song?

"This was Hrethel, after Herebeald was dead.
He couldn't bait the killer with blood-feud rules,
nor hate him for his wrongs. The murderer
was not his preferred son, but still, he was next
in the now blot-blurred line. Hrethel walked away
from the world, losing the plot, heart-tortured,
stone-faced. He marched alone into the flickering
light of God, leaving what he had left to leave:
2470 bones, strongholds, and cold sod to his sons,
as a rich man must.

106

"That old man was dust, but his old wars
remained. Swedes and Geats got in
each other's faces, and fought ferociously;
Hrethel dead, dark desires rising. Ongentheow's sons
banded together, full of war-wrath. On and on
they came, keeping no peace from overseas,
but twisting knives and words into ambush at
the hill of Hreosas. My own killer-kin avenged that,

2480   sing it with me, you all know the story, but there
was a cost: we lost Hæthcyn, Geat-lord,
in that bloodbath, and Hygelac,
my own Hygelac, drew his sword
the next morning. He brought it down
on Ongentheow, his brother's slayer,
splitting his helmet, sending the old Swede
to his death, drained, the dirt drinking his blood.
Even his leathern fists, feud-fortified,
failed in fending off his fate.

2490   "And me? I fought to repay the rings Hygelac
gave me, sword swift, debts edited in red.
He gave me greensward, rolling hills, a home of my own.
He had no need to seek any superhero among
the Gifthas, Swedes, or Spear-Danes, no hired merc
to secure his six. I was always there, his constant

companion, marching ahead, first to charge.

I was the soldier who kept my king shredding,

the warrior who kept his queen wed. I was his man, until—

Well. I'm not dead yet. I'll lead while taking

2500 my last breath, as long as this sword stands by, even if

I have to end with death. It's been my second in every battle,

since the very beginning, when I slew Dæghrefn,

the Hugas warrior, in a duel before both our armies.

He brought no hoard back to his ring-lord, that flag-waver,

but instead fell bravely, not to my blade, but to my boldness.

I wrung that man to death, my fists deep in his rib cage,

my hands in his lungs, his bone-vault broken.

Now I'll use all I have—sword, fists, sharpened edge,

honed heart—to engage the snake for this gold-heap."

2510 Beowulf blasted his last boast:

"I laid my life down on the daily when I was your age.

Now, gray guardian though I am, I'll show you

how it's done. I'll kill this creature if it's the last thing

I do. If it's no coward, it'll come out of its cave

and face its challenger."

He eyeballed each of his men, power-privileged

warriors, for the last time:

"I'd go in without weapons, as I always have,

if this weren't a dragon. I'd do it like a man, kill it

2520 barehanded, like I killed Grendel so long ago.

But mortal skin can't contend with a flame-spitting fiend,

and so I go in sword-armed, taking shield and mail-shirt.

I won't surrender when I see the beast, but fight it by the wall,

and God will dictate which brawler wins. Get a good seat, boys,

and look to the sky: your job's to watch this flier fall.

I'm decided, don't defy me. I've no more shade

to throw on this serpent-raider. Let the winner win,

let the loser get bent. My men, stay here

atop the barrow. Wait with your war-weapons.

2530 Watch and see who wins—who can suffer more,

who can be worse wounded, who can survive fire.

This is my fight. I don't ask for intervention—

none of you are strong enough to take this thing,

to try to stake your manhood on doing a dragon.

I'll be the one winning the gold, my bravery

the broadest, and if not, boys, this'll be

the battle that breaks your king."

Beowulf stood tall, his iron shield upraised, armored

in his own fame, his helmet, his mail-shirt, his faith

2540 firm only in Fate, a grit-god bearing brute weight,

beneath the rocky ledge. No trembling in his hands, but

a strong salute. He'd survived worse than this, a veteran

of foreign wars, of battle-betrayals, of heartbreak, flung

himself from cliffs over and over, surfaced singing.

There: a stone arch, and there a stream rushing from
the barrow's entry, a boiling geyser, furious fumes
and flames. No one could live long in there, not
without burning. Beowulf knew he couldn't fight
inside the hoard-lair. The dragon's heat was horrific.

2550 He worked his wrath into a roar. The main man of the
Weder-Geats bellowed into the blast zone, calling forth
his foe. Under the stone, warmth turned to war—
an echoed challenge bounced, and the dozing dragon
lifted her head, alert with fury. A human voice!
There'd be no negotiation, no settlement in metal.
Fire walked first, dragon's breath surging
out of the stones. Earth quaked as she rose
and roared in return. The challenging mortal
raised his shield as she emerged, a whipping wraith,
2560 a coil convulsing overhead, fangs, claws, and scales
railing against robbery, ready for war.
Beowulf's sword was already drawn, that razor edge,
that razing heirloom. Each of them, living, was
intolerable to the other, and in fury, they fell to it.

Feet planted, the people's provider held firm
behind his shield, even as the serpent swirled,
twisting and unfurling, her scales flame-swathed,

flinging herself hard at Fate, a flexing firework
aimed straight at the king. His shield shirked
2570 its duty, keeping him safe for only moments.
The famous warrior was, for the first time, naked.
Another first: Beowulf had never before been quarry,
God-snubbed, Fate-forsaken, his glorious, premeditated
victory unwritten. The Geat-lord raised a sooty fist
and punched in panic at armored scales, as his sword
slid, twisting against stony bones, his fang useless
against volcanic dangers. It dawned on the king
that he was afraid, his weapons forged without sorcery,
his defenses all man-made. The hoard-guard rippled
2580 in rage, her mouth a fusillade of flames, so furious
was she to feel even the dullest blade. Her war-lanterns
lit. Beowulf knew better than to expect victory.
His sword, unmatched until this hour, splintered
where it should've slain. His ageless iron
had never been conquered, but now?
Ecgtheow's son found himself engaged in ebbing:
loaded into a rattling cart and exiled
to a darker country, though unwilling
to go easy in the loss of long-held lodging.
2590 Everybody's gotta learn sometime.

Back at it again, the two battled furiously,
the dragon renewed, rapturous, inhaling,

111

uncoiling afresh. The man who'd been king
was wreathed in flame; he knew his end was near.
No one was coming, no seconds running to serve
or save him, no ring-raised warriors—those men,
that former family, were sprinting from his screams,
racing for safety, off the barrow and into the trees.

But one man felt something, a bond that bound him
2600 back. He was kin and could not leave his king
to die alone. His name was Wiglaf, and he was
Weohstan's son, that righteous warrior,
that Scylfing kinsman of Ælfhere.

Wiglaf watched his king writhe beneath
the heat of his flame-battered helmet,
remembering the rings that king had given him,
his comfortable home among the Wægmundings,
his halcyon holdings and heritage, come down
from his daddy. He could not run with the rest.
2610 He raised his linden shield and lifted his sword,
a blade with lineage of its own, a weapon come
from Eadmund, Ohthere's son, that exiled,
friendless one that Weohstan had killed
in combat. He'd borne his victim's arms
back to the dead man's kin: his engraved
helmet, woven chain mail, and sword,

giant-forged. Onela returned the gear,
ring-gift to a kin-killer, though slain Eadmund
had been his nephew. Weohstan held the hostile hoard
2620 for the rest of his life, helm, sword, shirt,
until his son came of age and needed metal
to prove his worth. When he was dying,
gray and aged, embarking into the unknown,
he showered Wiglaf in battle-bounty,
Geat-witnessed. Now was the young warrior's
first chance to align himself with his lineage,
to fight for his father and for his ring-lord.
He had a strong spirit, and his inheritance
was sharp as ever, a thing the serpent would learn,
2630 when soon they met.

Repulsed at their reluctance, Wiglaf sought
to convince his companions:
"Bro! Listen! Remember in the mead-hall,
we swore to our lord we'd stand by him,
swore to our ring-giver we were worth
his investment? That we'd bleed in our
battle-gear, given us for fighting, not strutting?
He favored us from among the flock,
gave us gifts, called us more than just mill-run
2640 warriors. I know he insisted he climb
this hill alone, the head of our country,

the best of men, but it's time for us to defy him!

Get in the zone. He's falling!

Do we watch him drop? No! Do we wait

for his heart to stop, for him to die? No!

Beowulf needs backup! On attack!

Let's save our savior from those flames!

I'd rather burn in a pyre alongside my ring-giver

than run home, arms untested against any enemy.

2650 My God, hear me!

It beggars belief that we wouldn't

even seek to slay this serpent, that we

wouldn't try to tear our prince from its teeth.

Men, I know, if you don't, he deserves better

than dragonfire, undefended

by his own. We're sworn to go together!

No? Well? Then I'm going in alone,

though my sword's nothing next to its skin.

I'll bring my king my shield, helmet,

2660 shirt, and sword."

He sprinted through fire, appearing armored

alongside his lord, shouting:

"Beowulf, I'm beside you! You'll dare to risk it all,

and fight to the finish, as you did when you were young.

You won't be bested while your heart beats!

Your fame won't diminish! Your history's here!

Be strong, my king! Your boy's with you in this fight.
Be your country's shield, as I battle on your right."

The dragon stanched any imminent surrender in herself.
2670 Her wrath rekindled, her own unearthly serpent song.
She brought forth fire, blasting it at those nuisance
humans, filthy, false-scaled, and intrusive.
She scintillated sword and shield, flash-burning
Wiglaf's lindenwood to ash.

His mail-shirt was like linen to her, so he ducked
under his kinsman's shield, still fighting. His king
shared that steel umbrella, once the young warrior
stood beside him, showered in sparks. Invigorated
by the thought of victory, the king used all his strength
2680 to strike, lunging at possibility. Nægling was the victim
of the swing, snapping like a straw. Beowulf's
blood-tested blade was wrecked by dragon skin.
It was not our man's wyrd to be assisted by sword,
no, not by sharp edges, nor ancient iron, and his
gray blade gave way under too strong
a swing, shattered by too straight a stroke.
Beowulf got no win from that weapon.

The third round sounded. The fire-breather
rallied, rocketing from her corner, and diving

2690 at that warrior, driving needle-fangs into his throat,
shaking him like a captured flag. Beowulf
went limp, his body wound-worn,
drenched in his own dark lifeblood.

Here's what I know: Wiglaf, Weohstan's son
saw his king collapsing, and showed his bloodline's
bravery and Geat-born grit. His fighting hand
was singed as he dodged the dragon's head,
but he drove lower, spurning safety to spit
the serpent's stomach with his ogre-etched sword.
2700 With that blade in her belly, she couldn't belch flame.
Her fires sputtered. Now Beowulf, with his last strength,
drew a dagger from his hip, a lethal hunting thorn,
and dipped it into the dragon's side, wounding her fatally:
blade met body, a bleak and bitter fight.

Together, these two slew their foe, courage conquering
flight, and that duo, kin by blood and bone, did it
side by side. Every warrior should step up to serve
his lord, throw down regardless of odds.
This was the last battle for the king, though,
2710 his final victory a grim one.

The old warrior's wounds wept the dragon's legacy:
scalding spit set by poisoned fangs, seething into sepsis.

Beowulf knew he was a goner. His chest heaved
with each heartbeat. He slumped against the wall,
doomed but dignified, admitting defeat,
easing his broken body down.
He fixed his eyes on the stone of the hall:
arches curving over tall columns, worked in an age
before he'd lived, by giants long gone under.
2720 And his new battle-brother, better than any of those others,
hand-washed his king's wounds, serving sweetness
even in this sorry state, unhelming him,
bathing him, bringing him peace.

Beowulf spoke, mortally wounded. Despite the doom
diminishing his light, he unlocked his word-vault. His time
was waning. His brain was all he had left; in it, an ultimate
ring-gift to bequeath. Death drew close and knelt beside him.

"If I'd ever had a son, I'd be giving him my armor now,
but I never fathered one, never gave my blood to an heir,
2730 and so this death is final. I'm the last of me.
I've been ruling here, fearless, for fifty winters.
I was the man. No neighbor came to war—my name
kept enemies at bay, and no one could scare me. I lived
in peace, and released my lease on battle, knowing
I had nothing to prove. I wasn't ambitious, never threw shade,
never took shit, never spat curses when I felt wronged,

117

but sat on the throne and weighed my people's woes
and wishes. I have to say, I did okay. Now, as I lie
dying, doomed by dragon, no one can claim I was a bad king.
2740 God can't call me a murderer, for I slew none of my kin.
My boy, get a move on, and bring your lord's last request.
I want to see what prize I won of this. Wiglaf, go under
that stone, past where the dragon lies, wickedly wounded,
her treasure targeted and taken. Climb into her hoard
and count my gold. Hurry. I want to hold it. I want to know
what I did, to look at my winnings, my gilded gifts,
the grave-goods of a gone people. I want to know it was worth it.
My dying will be easier if I see what I died to do:
garner a giant's treasure in exchange for my life.
2750 I'll let go then, of all my holdings,
my throne, my carefully guarded bones."

Bro, here's how the story goes: Weohstan's son
went directly, obeying without question
the command of his dying king. Still dressed
in heavy vines of mail, he ran to bring his man
satisfaction, ducking below the stony ledge, into
the barrow. He was victorious, battle-brightened,
and saw with shining eyes a trove of hoarded
Heaven, riches beyond compare, tapestries, piles of gold
2760 heaping the floor. That old moon-splicing serpent's lair

was full of ancient pitchers for pouring peace, goblets,
cups, corroding without women to offer them up. Helmets
red with rust, artfully twisted armbands without arms to hold—
and oh, all that old gold, so long concealed, so long inviolate,
wriggling back into the earth, despite the designs
of those who'd hidden it!

Wiglaf spied a standard, too, entirely woven of gold,
suspended on the wall over the rest, more delicately
wrought than any cloth he'd seen, glowing with illumination
2770 of its own, lighting the cave so he could inspect,
itemize the collection, imagine it emerging.
The dragon was gone entirely, no sign she'd ever slept
there, done to death by dagger, and driven
into darkness. Then, so I'm told, that man plunged
his hands into the hold, that ancient hoard of giant's gold,
and filled his arms with feast-gifts, plates, goblets,
anything, everything his heart desired, taking also
the standard, dragging the dragon's lantern down
from the wall. I mean, bro, the dragon was dead,
2780 the old king's swing had made that certain—
the one who'd guarded the glitz, who'd shown her love
by littering the land with abandoned homesteads
and burnt beds, who'd made midnight her inferno hour?
She'd been split into serpent skin.

Wiglaf made haste, driven by the treasure he carried,
hoping his lord would still be living, though he'd been
forced to leave him high and dry. He returned,
arms full of bounty, to find his king bleeding out,
pools of red, letting go of life. Wiglaf fell to his knees
2790 to drip water on the king's lips. The old man tried to speak,
and the knife-tip of a sentence stabbed from his locked
lung-vault. He stared at the gold, sorrowing.

"To God, the King, Eternal Throne-Holder,
I sing my thanks. That You've let me look on this
before I die, this gold, this get? It's enough.
My people lose me, but gain a hoard-gift.
Say that on the day of my dying, I went hard.
I traded my life for this. It's a good bargain.
My God, watch over my Geats. I'm going.
2800 These people are your people now. Shout
my last orders—tell my army to build a barrow
before my body blazes, one like the dragon had,
high up on the coast. I want it visible, towering
like a giant's tooth on Whales' Cape, so my people
know I was king, and so seafarers say my name
daily, nightly, call out 'Beowulf's Barrow!'

as they pass in their tall ships, bound here
over wild and misty waters."

The king unlatched his heavy golden collar,
2810 handing it off to his young defender,
giving him also his ornate helmet and war-shirt,
instructing him to wear them well.

"You're the end of the line, boy, the last standing
Wægmunding. Living has killed us all. We're dustbinned
by destiny. My courageous clan of noble men have gone
to ghost. Now I serve at their command."

Those were the warrior's last words. He had no more wisdom,
no more secrets, before he consigned himself to the pyre,
the final battle-fire for a body brutally broken. Beowulf's soul
2820 stepped from his breast to see what it could see.

It was agony for the would-be savior, so young, to see
his dear kinsman death-rattling on barren ground.

The dragon, that deep-dweller, lay dead as well, having done in
her enemy. She was limp and lifeless, her looping spine
and scales no longer lolling about piles of gold,
no longer ring-guarding. Keen-edged blades,

sweat-hammered and fervently filed, had bitten
her, broken her of soaring flight, ended her
adventures, leaving her stiff as a shovel-split
2830 snake, dead in dark dirt beside
a gilded grave. Never again   *So sad*
would she soar through a starry
sky, revel in rising rhapsody, rolling in and out
of clouds and mist, a raging rainbow, glinting golden.
She plummeted, Earth-struck, blunted in blissful
brutality by Beowulf. Hardly in history has there been
a man born, or so I'm told, who, brawny and brave
as men may be, would be able to battle such a one,
to throw himself into her biting breath, or even creep
2840 into her lair for fortune's sake, and fearlessly find
the treasure-keeper there, her eyes open, a wonder-ward.
The ancient hoard had changed ownership now, bought
by Beowulf's blood. Both he and his enemy had seen
the edge of existence, tripped and fallen over it.

It wasn't long before the forest-fled retainers
attempted to regain their status, those ten men
who'd run for the hills, abandoning their king
as the winged one was roaring in.
The cowards, who'd put their blades
2850 behind their backs when he'd needed

their strength, shambled out of the woods,
shields lifted, armor still on, to where the old king
lay collapsed. They found Wiglaf, crumpled beside him,
heartsick, his shoulder to the shoulder of his lord,
trying to wake him with water, but it was over.
There was no will left in Beowulf, no life-spark
to be ignited. God had decided, as He always does,
we all know it, and, bro, nobody changes God's mind.

The young warrior had words for them, though,
2860 terse words for the cowards who'd abandoned
their king. Wiglaf, Weohstan's son, spat severity
at the soldiers he'd found wanting.

"Anyone with half a brain's well aware that this king
treated us like princes, giving us gifts, the gear
that guards us even now. He opened his arms, offered all
who stood in his mead-hall armor: helmets, mail-shirts,
treasures. He treated us, his thanes, like sons, gave us
the glories he'd won, but, hey, I guess he had no judgment.
He threw those gifts away. What a fucking waste,
2870 in time of war, to armor and honor a corps of soldiers
who'd ignore him when he needed them most.
Our king had no cause to boast of his fight-family—
he never saw them fight. God allotted him a blow,
he forced his blade into the fray, braver than all

of you put together. I couldn't keep him safe,

defending his flank, but God gave me strength

to swing and help him. At least I, alone among these

ranks, tried. My sword sank in, the enemy

was injured, the dragon's fire-oaths

2880 dimmed, her advances weaker, but I couldn't save him.

Too few of you were loyal to our brave lord

in time of trouble. Well, kiss it all goodbye, boys,

those treasures you hoarded, those gifts,

those sparkling, unswung swords, the homes you held

by kindness of our king. That shit is gone.

Your families will founder. Your freeholds will fall,

the moment outland princes hear how you hid yourselves,

disgraced your king, and let him die undefended.

Are you warriors or weaklings?

2890 You should kill yourselves rather than live,

having dealt him this damage."

Wiglaf ordered that the battle's end be shouted out,

bad tidings brought to the men camped at the ridge,

retainers and unchosen warriors waiting heavyhearted

for reports. They'd spent the morning kneeling, nervous

for their beloved lord, expecting all and any outcomes:

king's death, or return of the king.

The messenger shouted truth, plainly, without hesitation.
The rider sped to the headland, forecasting for all to hear:

2900 "The people's prince, the Weders' lord and love,
the Geats' good gold-giver, is gone.
The king is dead. The dragon did him in,
but she's dead, too, stretched beside him,
an enemy slain by silver stabbing, a knife.
Beowulf's sword could not kill her, no matter
how he tried. Wiglaf is there now, with them both,
Weohstan's son, a survivor holding vigil for his dead,
a warriors' wake, for both the dear and the detested.

"Now. Listen up. War's coming for us,
2910 for this country. Soon our enemies will hear
our king's been killed. From sea to sea, everyone
from Franks to Frisians will mobilize.
Historic hatreds—the Franks have felt fury
since Hygelac led a flotilla of warships
into Friesland, though the Hetware held him there,
attacked him, and won with woeful odds.
Our leader, battle-dressed, was taken then,
his body falling, his army mourning.
He gave no winnings to his fighting force.
2920 The Merovingians haven't forgiven us.

"No kindness will come from the Swedes, either,
only vow-breaking, peace pacts poisoned.
Ongentheow, as everyone knows, slew Hæthcyn,
Hrethel's boy, at Ravenswood, back when the Geats
first attacked the battle-Scylfings. Vengeance was swift
for the Geat attack. Ohthere's father was ferocious,
a seasoned, elder general, and he slashed that seafarer,
Hæthcyn, and repossessed his own wife,
mother to both Ohthere and Onela, who'd been kidnapped,
2930 golden rings wrung from her fingers. Ongentheow
wasn't finished: he pursued his Geatish enemies,
driving them, panicked and bereft of their leader,
to Ravenswood, where he and his company
ran rings around the remnants,
reminding them how weak they were.
Through the black hours, he swore at them,
promising punishments, telling them
when the sun rose he'd shine his sword
on selected scalps, and string other soldiers
2940 from the gallows, make them treacle-sweets
for birds' beaks. But at dawn,
when they were despairing,
they heard the horn of Hygelac,

and that hero came for them,

following their trail with troops.

"The Swedes and Geats battled and plowed

a bloody path, identifiable for miles,

and no one, not even fools, could think them

finished fighting. The old man plotted murder,

2950 and made a move, retreating with his people.

Ongentheow knew higher ground would help him,

but he knew, too, that Hygelac was hard—

famous for his fight skills. The old man

couldn't hold long against the sea-warriors,

not while keeping his wife, children, and followers safe.

He dammed them in behind sheltering walls,

but Hygelac's men breached them, pouring

into the sanctuary like floodwater, drowning

camp and confines. Ongentheow stood firm,

2960 gray and proud, but he was trapped, surrounded

by swords, and Eofor was appointed

the Swede-king's judge and jury.

Wulf, Wonred's son, rushed the old man

in rage, and struck him so that blood soaked

his hair. Still, he did not back down,

but raised his own sword, and hacked,

harder than he'd been hit. The Swede-king

spun and struck, fighting for his people.
Wonred's son couldn't take him,
2970 brave Wulf though he was, and his blows
glanced off, until Ongentheow split his helmet
and forced him to flee, falling, head bloodied,
dazed though not dead. He was hurt, but he held,
and finally, his brother, Hygelac's loyal thane,
Eofor, lifted his own sword, an ancient piece
etched in ogre runes, and smashed it
into the old man's giant-forged helmet,
slashing past his shield. At last,
Ongentheow fell, the defender of his realm
2980 done and gone. Everyone ran to assist Wulf,
to bandage him, and carry him from the field,
now they were custodians of the bloody mud.
The walking warrior stripped Ongentheow
of his gear, his iron mail, his fierce sword,
his helmet, and ferried all this war-treasure
to Hygelac, who took the offering,
and said the giver would be repaid.
He told the truth, and for their courage,
Hrethel's heir, now king of Geats,
2990 gave Eofor and Wulf a hundred thousand
each in land-gifts and interlocked rings
of wealth to ratchet them up in status.
That was a good king.

None could critique his open hands.
He also gave over to Eofor
his only daughter, a bedmate
to bind him, a kin-bond
and vow of loyalty.

"So, to sum it up, the feud with the Swedes
3000 isn't over, and needs only this blood
to activate it again, a border-swarm,
a war walking into Geatland, the moment
they learn that Beowulf is gone. He's been
keeping us safe for decades, counting coffers,
battening the kingdom against invaders,
defending his citizens, and all the while
killing monsters, too. Come now, and hurry,
men, send him on his journey, pay him
our respects, and carry our king and ring-giver
3010 to his funerary rites. His pyre will be built—
heaped with gold for melting, which he won
with his life. The death-hoard is too heavy
for our hearts, and it will be burned
along with him who won it. That gold
isn't for decorating followers, not for starring
the bosoms of young women, or latching in memory
onto loyal throats. No. Now is a time for mourning,
for walking downcast the exile's road,

gray-garbed and grim, for the king is dead,
3020 his song is silence, his laughter and entertainment
forgotten. Take down your spears and touch
that dawn-chilled metal, raise them toward
a clouded world. No harp music will play
to call warriors in, but instead we'll waken
to the raven, a rush of black wings, telling in raw song
how she's watched the wolf and eagle worrying our dead,
carrion-clawed, competing over the feast."

That was the end of the forecast, and the augur
wasn't wrong. That messenger delivered it as evenly
3030 as such bad news can be delivered.

The troop was weeping, but they rose, and went
in woeful rows to Eagles' Cape, where, on the cold sand,
they found their king, soul long spent, that man
who'd given them everything he had,
whose rings had warmed their hands.
It was the end of his epic, the climactic close,
and Beowulf, their warrior-king, died mighty.
They saw beside him a wrathful wonder,
a sky-dragon become ground-ghost. That
3040 flame-spitter, scourge of those coasts,
had been scathed and sooted by her own song.
She was fifty feet long, she who'd ruled

in riving-rapture over their dreaming hours,
diving through dawns to nest with her treasure.
Now Death had won her. The wyrm would
no longer writhe with coins, but with worms.
Beside her lay the dragon's dowry:
grave-good goblets and cups,
dishes and knives, rust devouring them now,
3050 though they'd spent a thousand winters
serving the ghosts of powerful men.
There was a spell on the hoard,
left by a skeleton tribe, a ward
that said no man could touch it
unless God, Glory-Dispenser and Hoarder
of Humanity, chose a hero and gave permission
for the treasures to disperse.

What had he hoped, the man who'd pressed
his people's precious things into a cave beneath
3060 the cape? All his keeping came to nothing.
First, the dragon killed the king, then the king
killed the dragon. Maybe a man's mighty,
maybe he's known to all as a warrior, but
Death has his number. No one knows
when it'll be called, when he'll have to walk backward
out of the beer-hall, exiled from life. So it was for Beowulf,
when he sought battle in a barrow. Sure, the grave-guardian

was formidable, but our hero had no notion he was falling

out of Earth. The curse on that stony womb was set by men

3070 who'd impregnated it with treasure, claiming the confines theirs

until doomsday; if they couldn't possess them, no one could.

Any man who thieved was fated to perish, pushed

into pagan places, punished forever.

Beowulf never imagined gold could bring grief.

He forgot: not all gifts are for getting.

Wiglaf, Weohstan's son, took the floor:

"One man slipped down this slope, he alone deciding,

but we rest are roped to him: many will suffer

similar fates now. No counselor could convince

3080 our king, our old and beloved protector,

that he shouldn't come at the guardian of this gold,

but instead let her dream unmolested, drowsing

alongside her beloved hoard, ground-nested,

until world's end. Beowulf's fate was written, too.

He opened the barrow and showed us its bounty,

but he paid in blood and bone—his destiny

was too tempting, and it drew him here.

I've been inside, counted treasures heaped

in the dark, given my ticket to voyage, solitary,

3090 under tons of soil. I heaved a heap of heart-won gold

into my arms, precious beyond compare, and bore it here,

to share it with my king. I carried all this treasure

to where Beowulf could view it. He was alive then,
though fading. He listed his longings,
his last commands, bade me welcome you,
man by man, and bid you build a barrow
great enough to justify his gifts and his going.
He wanted a memorial built to last, to light the future,
because of all men who've ever lived, he was the strongest,
3100 and the bravest, and the brightest, and the best.
Now come with me. Let us look on the treasure
together, piled against the wall. I'll lead you
to the dragon's lair and show you, up close,
the golden ornaments, so you'll know
what your king died for. Meanwhile,
let the bier be readied, so when we emerge
we can carry Beowulf to it, lay him upon our love,
and send him to his new hall,
under the throne of the Lord."

3110 Weohstan's son, courageous as ever, ordered heroes
and hall-holders to the forest, to chop logs
and splinter trees. All those men, with men of their own,
collected kindling for the king.

"Now he'll be consumed. Let a white and brilliant flame
catch our leader. Let the fire take him, our famous man,
who fought off slings and arrows, who battled armies,

who never backed down. At last, a shaft sounded his depths,

pursuing the barb as it primed his heart,

feathers fanning across his breast."

3120 The son of Weohstan summoned seven

of the best men to descend again into darkness,

and went alongside them, the eighth man,

entering that cursed place. One soldier,

the man in front, carried a light.

No one sought to gamble or grab.

The guard was gone and the challenge

was pointless. They carried it all out,

dazzle-draped, a heaving hoard of gore-bought

gold, unprotected, and piled it in public.

3130 It was easy to enact their leader's last wish.

Then they heaved the dragon over the cliffs

into the sea, brine-bedding that beast-bride,

that ring-taker. The endless accursed treasures

they stacked on a cart, and bore them

with their dead leader, his skin gone gray

as a barnacle, to Whales' Cape.

The Geats began the pyre, howling over

Beowulf, their best brother, hanging hoard-helmets

about it, shields and steel-shirts, as he'd insisted.

3140 They placed him in the center of all this treasure,
their lost love, and built a bone-fire worthy
of men's ends. Storm-smoke shuddered
from the blaze thick and dark, and the flames
keened louder than any man's weeping.
The whipping winds momentarily stilled,
until Beowulf's heart-helm broke. His bones
blackened as his boys bellowed their grief.

Then another dirge rose, woven uninvited
by a Geatish woman, louder than the rest.
3150 She tore her hair and screamed her horror
at the hell that was to come: more of the same.
Reaping, raping, feasts of blood, iron fortunes
marching across her country, claiming her body.
The sky sipped the smoke and smiled.

The Geats got down to it, driving the materials
of the memorial into a mound, a promontory
crowned with Beowulf's marker, lit so sailors
could see it from afar. Ten days it took to make
their hero's new home. It contained, walled up,
3160 the remnant of his hoard-gold, wrought to remain
long after Geats were gone. Rings of kings,
and torcs, jewels clouded with black smoke,
the dragon's darlings—and before her, that lost tribe's,

a trove of treasure trespass-cursed from out of earth,
now gone to ground again. They covered it over
with gravel, and I hear it's there still, a leftover lament,
lacking living hands for spending.

Twelve thanes, battle-tested sons of worthy men,
took themselves to horseback and coursed
3170 around the tomb, weeping, wringing
the old songs from their tongues, dirge-chanting,
telling the legend of Beowulf, their king.
His courage, his fury, his wars.
They did all this grieving the way men do,
but, bro, no man knows, not me, not you,
how to get to goodbye. His guys tried.
They remembered the right words. Our king!
Lonely ring-wielder! Inheritor of everything!
He was our man, but every man dies.
3180 Here he is now! Here our best boy lies!
He rode hard! He stayed thirsty! He was the man!
He was the man.

ACKNOWLEDGMENTS

In 2017, I was nominated for a World Fantasy Award, and two of the award jurors, Betsy Mitchell and Elizabeth Engstom, attended a reading at which I read from *The Mere Wife* and talked about my research for the novel, the translations of *Beowulf* I'd read, and the ways in which late nineteenth- and early twentieth-century translations by men had shaped our understanding of the female characters in the poem. During the Q&A, they asked when my translation would be out. I laughed and said there wouldn't be one—I wasn't qualified—and both jurors laughed back and said it sounded like I was as qualified as many of the other people who'd translated it over the years. "Qualified," to my mind, meant I'd certainly need a PhD, perhaps a Nobel Prize. This perception, obviously, didn't come from nowhere. Despite the significant work of female and other marginalized scholars, despite several excellent translations by women, the fact remains that *Beowulf*, at least for publication, has longstandingly been aggressively marketed as an off-limits area. I'd adapted it into a novel, but somehow it still seemed off-limits for me to dig into the actual poem. Well, fuck that. The notion of *Beowulf* through the lens of the bro-story had been rattling around in my head for a decade. I took the idea to a writing retreat a few weeks later and pitched it to a group of fire-breathers: Kelly Link, Amal el-Mohtar, Brooke Bolander, Sarah McCarry, Libba Bray, Holly Black, Caitlyn Paxton, Catherynne Valente, Ysabeau Wilce, Kat Howard, and Annalee Flower Horne, and they had the faith I wasn't sure I had. In the scholarly realm, I owe special thanks to Carolyne Larrington, who generously invited me to Oxford University to read from the in-progress translation, and to Emily Wilson, with whom I had a public conversation about her own translation of *The Odyssey* in the summer of 2018, and whose comments on both translation and translator's perception inspired and informed this work.

I owe specific thanks to every woman who's ever published a translation of *Beowulf*—I read as many of those translations as I could over the course of working on this one. As well, I pored over everything from Clara Thomson's 1899 *Adventures of Beowulf*, a detailed paraphrase for English schoolchildren, to William Morris's glitteringly bonkers 1896 experiment in archaically toned berserkery; Burton Raffel's 1963 verse translation; Marijane Osborn's 1983 verse translation; Seamus Heaney's 1999 verse version; Meghan Purvis's 2013 translation, which breaks the book-length poem into a series, enabling voices once muffled beneath the original's narrative umbrella to be realized; and the *Beowulf By All* project, spearheaded by Elaine Treharne, for which more than two hundred translators each translated fifteen lines—I read and learned from them all as I worked on this. Particularly of help and inspiration to this translator: articles and essays by Catherine A. M. Clarke, David Clark, Kevin Kiernan, Carolyne Larrington, Clare A. Lees, Adam Miyashiro, Toni Morrison, Marijane Osborn, Gillian R. Overing, and Elaine Treharne. Kiernan's "Grendel's Heroic Mother" was my introduction to the notion of Grendel's mother as Germanic heroine (which helped inspire *The Mere*

Wife), and from there, I considered the rest of the women of the poem using similar standards. The poets Danez Smith, Miller Wolf Oberman, Jos Charles, and Anne Carson inspired me with their takes on notions of the epic, and with their transformations of similar materials, and I thank them for providing the light during some inevitable moments of darkness.

I owe great thanks to my team on this book: my editor Sean McDonald at Farrar, Straus and Giroux and MCD, who said yes to this, as well as my editor Marika Webb-Pullman at Scribe Publications, and everyone at Scribe. At FSG and MCD × FSG, special thanks to Daniel Vazquez, Brian Gittis, Carrie Hsieh, Nina Frieman, Songhee Kim, Ellen Feldman, Logan Hill, and Debra Fried, and to Keith Hayes for the magnificent cover, and at MacMillan Audio, thanks to Robert Allen, Tom Mis, and Steve Wagner for shepherding this book into the version I wrote it to be—something a person might play loud. Thanks as well and as ever to my agent, Stephanie Cabot, who for ten years has been telling me I can do whatever I set my mind to doing, and to the entire Gernert Company team, including Ellen Goodson Coughtrey, Rebecca Gardner, Anna Worrall, and Will Roberts for believing in this ever-more-twirling dragon of a career. Thanks once more to the heroic Beowulf Sheehan, who took the magnificent author portrait with assistance from Sami Schneider, and to Mandy Bisesti and Greg Purnell, whose makeup and barbering made me look proper.

Gratitude to China Miéville, who's volunteered his extraordinary brain to my service for nearly a decade. Gratitude to Matthew Wimberley, who was willing not only to read this in manuscript but also to listen to a long audio file in which I muttered this into my phone. Deep thanks as well for supports both mental and material to Cindy and Bill Badger, Kurt and Kat Badger, Jim Batt, Jess

Benko, Kim Boekbinder, Brooke Bolander, Chris Bolin, Mike Brand, Tammy Brand, Alexander Chee, Matt Cheney, Molly Crab-apple, Kate Czajkowski, Kelley Eskridge, Isaac Fitzgerald, Jeffrey Ford, Craig Franson, Larisa Fuchs, Neil Gaiman, Nicola Griffith, Adriane Headley, Mark Headley, Molly Headley and Idir Bencaci, Benjamin Henry, Mary Hickman, Dani Holtz, Coco Karol, Doug Kearney, Joseph Keckler, Alice Sola Kim, Meghan Koch, Ben Loory, Carmen Maria Machado, Juan Martinez, Téa Obreht, Erin Orr, Amanda Palmer, Hadrien Royo, Frances Schenkkan, Joshua Schenkkan, Sarah Schenkkan, Jesse Sheidlower, Sxip Shirey, Elizabeth Senja Spackman, Danielle Trussoni, Ann VanderMeer and Jeff VanderMeer, Henry Wessells.

Most profound gratitude and love go to William Badger, my in-house maker of magic, who over the course of my work on this translation read perhaps ten drafts, going over every line to the extent that he, too, began dreaming in Old English; brought me rhymes, reversals, and corrections I'd never have found on my own; and, as if that were not enough, also embarked on the epic quest of having a baby with me. Grimoire gets the dedication of this book, but the fact that this translation got done while I was pregnant and during the first year of Grim's life is in large part due to Will's work.

Thank you, finally, to those encountering *Beowulf* for the first time through this version, the teachers teaching it, the librarians recommending it, and the scholars shaking things up, enabling works like this translation to find their place on the shelves. You are the warriors in my home-hall, the wolves in my favorite fens, and the gold in my hoard.